An Impossible Attraction

An Impossible Attraction

A Cavallo Brother Romance

Elsa Winckler

TULE
PUBLISHING

Chapter One

"THANK YOU FOR the offer, but I decline," Zoe said, trying to ignore the quivering in her stomach. Why the blasted man always had this effect on her, even over the phone, she didn't know, but it was driving her crazy.

It was early December and she still had a lot of work to finish before the Christmas break. The last thing she had time for was talking to Dale Cavallo. She'd been working since early this morning and had been sending out quotes when his call came through and now she had to waste precious minutes with him.

"You don't think your reaction is a tad childish?" Dale's voice filled her ear, sending a tremble down her spine as it always did.

"Me, childish?" she snapped. "Childish is the perfect word to describe your behavior last Tuesday. You summoned me to meet you at the site of your new hotel in the middle of nowhere. I had to leave everything I was busy with and fly out there. And then? I was there for the entire day and you never once spoke to me! Your brother showed me around. Believe me, I got the message that the whole idea to use me as interior designer was not yours."

"When exactly should I have talked to you?" Dale asked, his voice cool. "While you were yelling at my bother for some ridiculous reason or other, or when you sat sulking at lunch?"

Zoe inhaled sharply. She didn't think of herself as a violent person, but if Dale were here, she would damn well clobber him! She didn't want to work for him. He was just too damned arrogant, too sure of himself, too male, too bloody everything.

Clutching her phone with tense fingers, she counted to ten. Nope, she was still spitting fire. She tried to inhale again but couldn't get any air through the stiffness in her throat. The man made her so mad!

"Let's leave your brother and my sister out of this discussion," she said, and tried to calm herself. She was not going to defend her actions. "I will not be able to do the interior decorating of your new hotel. Thank you for offering me the job; I hope you find someone else."

And then she did something she had never done before. She slammed the phone down without saying good-bye.

Still steaming, she got up from behind her desk but before she could move, Susan, her second-in-charge in the business, poked her head around the door.

"Everything okay? Difficult client?"

Zoe tried a calming breath. "Something like that. Can I help?"

"Can we talk about the job in Paarl?" Susan asked, and Zoe nodded, showing Susan to the chair in front of her desk.

Usually, she was excited about new projects, and this new development near the beautiful town of Paarl was something she'd been dreaming of getting involved with. Drat the bloody Cavallos. Ever since her sister had met the oldest brother, they seemed to be everywhere.

Yes, they were all drool-worthy but, from the moment Dale Cavallo had pinned her down with his coffee-brown eyes in his mother's restaurant in Cape Town, he'd managed to turn her into a babbling idiot.

That orchestrated lunch at Rosa's had been one of her mother's not-so-subtle attempts to get her sister Caitlin and Don Cavallo back together. Dale had phoned her just a day or so before with the offer to do the work for them and even over the phone he'd sounded surly. So, when he'd barely acknowledged her at the lunch, she hadn't been surprised.

She had wanted to ignore him, but the minute their eyes met, something deep inside her had been touched, and she didn't like the feeling.

It was as if her body had simply taken over her brain. Her heartbeat went up several notches, her hands were sweaty, her mouth dry. She had been so upset—never before had a man reduced her to such a state that she couldn't see straight.

Yes, he was drop-dead gorgeous and very, very, very sexy. Whoever first coined the phrase tall, dark, and handsome had probably seen the Cavallo brothers together. But although she could acknowledge his brothers were also very attractive, very sexy, she didn't respond to them in the same way.

Why her reaction to Dale was like that of a sex-starved spinster, she had no idea. At twenty-seven she was no spinster and okay, yes, she couldn't remember the last time she'd had sex, but she wasn't starved, for goodness' sake.

She simply had to ignore him, and now that she'd declined his offer, it was only a matter of time.

"What do you think?" Susan's voice finally penetrated her thoughts.

Zoe leaned over and took the plan Susan held in front of her. She had work to do and thinking about Dale Cavallo making her weak in the knees was not helping. Oh, hell, that was not what she was thinking, was it? He irritated her, he was overbearing, and he was insufferable.

She had to try and remember that.

TWO DAYS LATER, Dale was still trying to figure out why he wasn't more pleased with the whole outcome. He had so much work and he'd been in his office since early this morning, but he hadn't been able to finish anything yet. Zoe Sutherland was on his mind and he was struggling to focus on his work.

She was right. It hadn't been his idea to ask her to do the

interior design and decorating of their new hotel. He grimaced. To tell the truth, since he'd met her, he didn't have a rational thought in his body. Which was the single most important reason to steer clear of any involvement with the leggy brunette.

She'd turned him on even before he'd seen her for the first time. The sound of her voice over the phone had caught him completely off guard. His reaction disturbed him to such an extent he told his brother he wasn't interested in working with her. He didn't want to see the girl to whom the sexy, throaty voice belonged.

Getting seriously involved with a woman was simply not part of his future. So, when just the sound of a strange woman's voice had him wondering about her, he knew to stay away.

He got up from behind his desk and walked to the big windows overlooking Cape Town. This hotel had been his first project when he'd joined his brothers in the business. When he'd seen this particular piece of land, he'd immediately been able to see the finished building in his mind's eye—lots of glass to reflect the mountain, the sea, the blue skies.

The building had been a talking point in the architectural world. Since then, he'd tried to emulate the same feel in most of the other hotels he designed.

And he'd designed the hotel in such a way that guests would be able to experience the city's two main attractions—

Table Mountain, one of the new seven wonders of the modern world on the one side, and the harbor and the sea on the other.

But today, the mountain's usual powerful and charismatic pull failed to enchant him like it usually did and he stared out towards the harbor, his gaze following a ship as it was leaving. He wished it was that easy to forget about Zoe.

It was an ordinary Sunday the first time he had seen her. His mother had invited them all for lunch at her restaurant. And there they were. All three Sutherland sisters and a friend, Dana, if he remembered correctly. All four of them stunning, but his eyes had zoomed in on just one of them. And he'd known even before they were introduced which sister she was. Zoe. The one with the voice.

He had seen Caitlin before and she was a stunner, so he should have expected her sisters to be as gorgeous. But he wasn't prepared for Zoe. At all. She was wearing a simple turquoise top and a short, white skirt showed off her long, tanned legs. He was a leg-man, always had been. And Zoe's legs had nearly brought him to his knees.

He didn't remember much else about the day. Except sitting next to her, listening to her voice, absorbing her scent. He'd been like a lovesick schoolboy, for crying out loud. He'd walked away that day with every intention of staying away from her. She was the kind of woman who could ruin a man.

There was a knock on his door and his younger brother

David walked into his office. They normally shared one big office, but they also each had a smaller one they used when they were seeing clients or when, like today, he didn't need his brothers' constant bantering.

"Don says Zoe declined your offer to do the interior of the hotel near the Kruger National Park?" David said.

Irritated, Dale shrugged. "It wasn't my idea to use her to begin with. It was Don's suggestion."

"I hear she's very good at what she does."

"Well, I don't trust strangers with my plans, so it's just as well," Dale said. "And you saw her at the site last week— she's a bloody spitfire, and I don't need that kind of aggravation in my life."

David laughed. "Well, she thought Don was cheating on her sister—in her shoes, you'd react the same way. So, what's really bothering you? That she's too sexy?"

Dale quickly looked at his brother.

"Yes, I think she's sexy, don't you?" David grinned.

Dale opened his mouth to deny it but realized it would be useless. Zoe was stunningly beautiful. But he didn't like the idea that his brother thought her sexy.

"Yes, she's beautiful. All the more reason I'm happy she declined the offer."

David cocked his head. "Is this because of that intern who worked for you early last year? What was her name again? Tammy, Sammy? The one who used your plans to enter a competition? The one you had a thing for?" He grinned.

Dale scowled. "Don't remind me. I still can't believe how gullible and foolish I'd been. I'd let myself be duped by a pair of baby blues and a dimple—not a mistake I intend to make again."

When Tammy had asked to take the plans of a new hotel home with her, he hadn't hesitated. She was working for them and, yes, he'd been sleeping with her.

Fortunately, a friend of his who had been on the selection committee of the competition recognized the plan as Dale's work and contacted him. Dale had been in time to stop the process, but the whole incident left a bad taste in his mouth and left him distrustful of women in general and of people who wanted to use his work in particular.

David laughed. "It's called lust, my dear brother, and that usually clouds the brain."

"Don't I know it. What that lesson taught me is to stay clear of career-driven, beautiful women who will do anything to advance themselves."

"The Sutherland women are gorgeous, I have to agree, but I've heard very good things about Zoe's firm," David said. "I don't think you can accuse her of sleeping her way to the top."

"Look, just leave it, okay? I'm the architect and I've done all the interior decorating of our hotels up until now. I don't see why I have to involve a stranger just because our brother is sleeping with her sister. And, yes, I know her firm is doing well, but frankly, power-hungry women scare the living daylights out of me. And I can't help wondering—whose idea was it to offer her the job? Don's or hers?"

"You're not making any sense," David said. "She declined your offer remember?"

"Yeah, probably after she realized she won't be able to wrap me around her little finger."

David slapped him on the back. "Sounds to me like that's exactly what she's been doing!" He grinned as he left the office.

Scowling, Dale stared after his brother. Damn it, he had to get this bloody woman out of his mind. He still remembered in vivid detail how she'd looked when she ripped into Don last week. Her sapphire eyes had been spitting fire, and all Dale could think about was how it would be to unleash all that passion in a bedroom. His bedroom.

That was the reason he'd ignored her for the rest of the day. Because speaking to her meant he had to look at her. And every time his eyes met hers, all he wanted to do was cart her off to the nearest bed. So, instead of being friendly, he'd behaved like an insufferable fool.

Restlessly, he stared at his phone while an idea kept swirling around in his head. Finally, he smiled and reached for the instrument. There was a way to get one particular Sutherland away from Cape Town and regular family meetings. Their new hotel in London was supposed to be his next project, but he had enough to keep him busy over here.

It would be very good exposure for Zoe's firm and, most importantly, she'd be in another country. By the time she returned, he'd be over this silly thing he had for her, and life would return to normal.

ZOE SAT UP in bed and touched her cheeks. They were wet. She switched on the light and got out of bed. It was still very early, but she was not going to sleep again. Not after the dream she'd just had.

Fed up with herself, she walked towards the kitchen. She was twenty-seven, for goodness' sake. Surely she should be over the fact her father had left them when she was still in school.

She put on the kettle, got out the coffee. It was this business with Dale that probably triggered the whole thing again. It left her unsettled.

Why, after all this time, she still remembered the day her dad had left, she didn't know. They had all been doing homework and he'd called them to come and say good-bye. At first she thought he was going on one of his many trips. But that particular time the suitcase was much bigger, and his smile hadn't quite reached his eyes.

She didn't remember what he said. But she did remember how she felt—that somehow if she'd been different, if she'd been better, he would not have left.

Her phone rang. It was Hannah. Smiling, she answered.

"Hi, Sis, it's so nice to hear from you! Where are you?"

"Still in New York," Hannah said.

"You sound tired."

"That I am," Hannah said. "Oh, my goodness, Zoe, I'm sorry. I only now realized the time. It must still be very early on your side of the world and you were probably still sleeping after a date with … who is the new man in your life again? Stephen? Is that the right name? Or is it Bruce? Or is Bruce the guy you dumped earlier this year? You go through them so quickly, I'm never sure," Hannah teased.

"It could have been Stephen, I'm not sure. I'm not with anyone at the moment."

"Hmm, so he lasted two whole months, if I'm not mistaken. You ditched him again before he could ditch you?"

Zoe sighed. "He was getting annoying."

Hannah was quiet for a few seconds. "You never date a guy long enough to let him do the ditching."

"We know firsthand that men don't stick around, don't we?"

"That is unfortunately true. Just don't forget that you're a beautiful, smart woman. Any man would be lucky to have you."

Zoe looked down at herself and smiled. "Thank you for saying that, although if you could see me now…" She giggled.

"Send me a picture. I miss sitting around in pyjamas with my sisters," Hannah said. "Anyway, I'm phoning to congratulate you. Caitlin seems to be still dating Don Cavallo and she tells me you're going to do the interior decorating for the Cavallos' new hotel. The one they're planning to build near the Kruger National Park."

"Well, then Caitlin hasn't spoken to her boyfriend today. I've declined the offer."

"Why would you do that? This is a great opportunity for you, Zoe."

"There is no way I can work with him. He is just too damn annoying, too overbearing, too bossy, too… male."

"Well, if you put it like that…" Hannah said, giggling.

"I love what I do and I'm at the point in my business where I can decide with whom I want to work. And I definitely don't want to work with Dale Cavallo. Ever. But please, let's talk about something else. So, will you be home for Christmas? We haven't seen you in ages."

Hannah laughed. "I've never heard someone change the topic so quickly. But okay, yes, I'm coming home for a week over Christmas. I haven't seen you guys since…" She trailed off.

Zoe grimaced. Damn it, they couldn't talk about anything without mentioning the bloody Cavallos. "When we had to sit through a lunch with the Cavallos at their mother's restaurant. We all had to be nice to them because Caitlin liked the oldest one."

"Don't remind me," Hannah growled. "If Caitlin decides to keep Don, we'll probably be forced to do that often."

They talked for a few more minutes before Caitlin said good-bye. Frowning, Zoe put down the phone. She had to try and get away for a while. Hannah was right—between their mother and Rosa, the Cavallos' mother, hardly a week went by without a get-together of the two families. And if she wanted to get Dale Cavallo out of her mind, she had to find a reason not to see him.

All her instincts were warning her not to get involved with him in any way. The one time in her life she'd ignored these voices, she'd been hurt. Well, okay, her pride had probably been more hurt than anything else, but still.

She'd met George in college. He was captain of the varsity rugby team, handsome, and paid her just enough compliments to turn her head to mush.

When she'd decided to pay him a surprise visit and found him in bed with another woman, it had finally dawned on her—if her own father hadn't even stayed with her, why would any other man find something in her to make him stay? So, after that disaster, she never dated a man for too long and she made sure she sent him on his way before he found a reason to leave her.

And normally, she'd forget the guy quickly. But something was telling her Dale Cavallo would not be so easy to put out of her mind. She hadn't been able to stop thinking about him ever since she'd met him.

Fed up with herself and her thoughts, she grabbed her coffee and walked back to her room. Why was she still thinking about the damn man?

SUSAN WALKED INTO her office just as Zoe was putting the phone down. She wanted to jump up and down. What wonderful news on this beautiful morning.

Dramatically, Susan shaded her eyes. "Wow, what a brilliant smile! I haven't seen you smiling like that in ages. Have you won the lottery?"

Zoe laughed. "Even better!" She pointed to the phone. "I just had a call from the spokesperson of a newly renovated hotel on the outskirts of London. He's offered us the job to do the interior decorating for the whole hotel."

"But that's wonderful news, Zoe. Especially because you turned down the Cavallo's offer to work on their hotels." There was a hint of reproach in Susan's voice.

Zoe ignored her. Susan had been stunned when Zoe had told her they would not be doing the Cavallo job. But fortunately, because it was her business, she didn't have to explain her decisions.

"How did they know about us? One would think there are more than enough interior decorators in London."

"I haven't even asked, I was so happy with the offer," Zoe said. "But you remember the smaller job we did there last year? They probably heard about us from them."

"When do they want us to start? And who will you send?"

"I'll be going myself," Zoe said immediately. "They want us to start in the beginning of March next year."

Zoe couldn't stop smiling. She'd been looking for a chance to get away, and this was a great opportunity for her firm and also a lovely excuse not to have to do the Sutherland-Cavallo thing for a while. It couldn't have come at a better time.

Chapter Two

Two months later

IT WAS A magical evening. Zoe swallowed against the lump in her throat. Her sister was now married to Don Cavallo. She still couldn't quite get her head around the idea that one of her sisters was a married woman. But there was no doubt Caitlin was ecstatically happy—she hadn't seen her without that huge smile all day.

The wedding reception was being held in the Cavallo's luxurious boutique hotel on Mahé, one of the beautiful islands of the Seychelles. As far as settings went, one could hardly find a more romantic, fairy-tale venue for Caitlin and Don's wedding.

The bridal couple were dancing. The music changed, the lights dimmed. Don pulled her sister closer to him, smiled down at Caitlin, and she simply beamed. Her sister made such a beautiful bride.

Hannah leaned across to Zoe. "Our sister looks so happy." She sighed. "Though I still can't believe she decided to marry the guy. Christmas morning we were all still footloose and fancy-free and by the next morning, we had a sister who was engaged to be married!"

"And two months later, we're at their wedding!" Zoe giggled.

"But will it last?" Hannah said, her eyes on the couple. "What do you think?"

Zoe shook her head. "I wish I knew. How realistic is it to think you can love only one person for the rest of your life? Some animals mate for life, but from what I've seen, humans struggle with the concept."

Hannah sighed. "Yep, sad but true."

Male laughter reached them and Zoe's heart lurched; her hands became clammy. Next to her, Hannah stiffened. That meant Dale Cavallo and his two other brothers were back at the table.

She and Hannah stared at the wedding couple for a few minutes. Don pulled their sister even closer and kissed her forehead before he cuddled her close.

"Caitlin believes true love is possible," Hannah said. "She has apparently even conquered her trust issues and believes Don would never be unfaithful."

"I know, and I hope she's right."

Dana, Caitlin's best friend, who was the other bridesmaid, pulled her chair up and moved her head slightly in the direction of the three Cavallo brothers. "We've probably danced with every man at the wedding. Every man except them, that is. And they, in turn, have danced with every woman out there, except with us. Strange, don't you think?"

she asked.

"This is probably the last dance, the evening is drawing to a close, so hopefully we won't have to dance with them at all." Hannah just about snarled.

Zoe looked at her watch. She was very glad the evening was nearly over; she was tired of trying not to look in Dale Cavallo's direction.

The last time she'd seen him was on Christmas Day, and he'd actually been quite civil. Probably because his mother had been around. But today, he'd been glaring at her ever since she and her sisters walked down the aisle earlier.

The groom and his three groomsmen waiting for the bride had been a sight to behold. All four of them were tall, dark, and sexy, and she could swear the testosterone levels around them rose by the minute in the small chapel.

That was when she'd noticed Dale's eyes on her. And realized he'd been scowling. What had she done? Yes, she'd turned down his request, but that had been months ago, and this was a wedding, for goodness' sake.

And damn it, why her hormones jumped to attention every time she saw him, she had no idea. Her body's reaction to the man was downright embarrassing. Good heavens, it was not as if he was the first attractive man she'd ever seen. But even just a glimpse of the man was sufficient stimulation for her hormones to produce so much saliva she worried every time that she'd start drooling over him.

"So, Dale, you're the second oldest, when are you getting married?" David grinned.

Irritated, Dale looked at his brother. He swore and grabbed his glass of wine. "Don't be ridiculous."

"Well, you've been staring at Zoe all night long, I was just wondering." David sniggered.

He glared at David. "I'm not staring." When his eyes returned to Zoe's back immediately, he realized how ridiculous he sounded. But then, ever since Zoe Sutherland had walked into his life, he'd been doing ridiculous things.

"I don't know how you think that, David," Darryn, their other brother, said. "You've been staring at Dana all night."

David's grin widened. "What's not to stare at? They're all beautiful."

"I don't know about Dana, but Dale, I'll tell you what I told Don—stay away from the Sutherland women. They're trouble." Darryn had the usual scowl when the Sutherland sisters were mentioned.

"So that's why you can't keep your eyes off Hannah?" Dale was glad he could shift attention away from him. "Because you're trying to stay away from her?"

Darryn glowered at him. "Don't be an idiot," he said in a clipped voice.

Feminine giggles floated over to them, and Dale turned to stare at the three bridesmaids sitting on the other side of the table. They watched the dancing. Dana was beautiful, David was right. And so was Hannah. But it was Zoe to whom his eyes kept returning, no matter how many times he tried to look away.

"Oh, look. Caitlin's mom is on her way over. I've never seen anyone her age with so much energy." David waved at the smiling older woman walking in their direction.

Her face lit up when she saw them and she rushed closer.

HANNAH LOOKED OVER Zoe's shoulder. She cussed under her breath and grabbed her bag.

"Oh, hell, Mom is on her way. I'm going to the ladies' room…" But Hannah was too late. Their mother swooped down on them and waved to the three brothers behind them.

"Why aren't you young people dancing?" She laughed. "It's a wonderful night, you're young, all gorgeous, come on!" She motioned for the three men to get up.

She bent down and whispered to them, "Bridesmaids are supposed to dance with the groomsmen at least once, you know. Especially if they look like those three! Come on, girls, bat those eyelashes." Her eyes twinkled. "Haven't I taught you anything?" She ended on a loud whisper.

Zoe closed her eyes and wished the floor would swallow her up. She loved her romance-writing mother dearly but, at times like this, Zoe could cheerfully throttle her. She was forever trying to find husbands for her daughters. Zoe hoped now that Caitlin was married, her mother would back off, but obviously she had no such plans.

Smiling, her mother waved at them and moved away. The music changed again, and the next minute Dale stood in front of her, holding out his hand for a dance. Zoe glanced towards Hannah and Dana, but the other two Cavallos held out their hands towards her sister and their friend as well.

There was no way she could refuse this dance—her mother would never forgive her. Okay, she'd do this and then nobody could accuse her of not behaving properly.

This was such a bad idea, but short of causing a scene, she couldn't say no. She took a deep breath and, without looking at Dale, put her hand in his—her last rational act.

The next minute Dale had her on her feet and spun her around. Then he pulled her in and kept her close to his body as he danced around the floor with her. Her feet followed his as if she'd done this a million times before, as if they'd always been dancing together. His movements were flawless, graceful, intoxicating.

This close to him, his scent filled her nostrils, seeped through her skin into her bloodstream from where it filled every cell in her body. His powerful muscles flexed under her hands, his breath caressed her check, and his big, warm hand stroked her sensuously up and down her bare back, leaving every centimetre of her flesh craving more. Their bodies were fused together. She closed her eyes and let the music and the man take over.

This would end in a few minutes; she would probably not see Dale again very soon, if ever, but for the moment she was tired of denying herself this sensation.

Desperately, she tried to get her sluggish brain cells to work, tried to rationalize what she was feeling. If she thought about it, her reaction was normal. She was young and unattached; he was a sought-after, rich tycoon—what girl wouldn't swoon a little bit? And anyway, this was probably the way he always danced with any woman. She'd read enough about him to know he seldom had the same girl on his arm. So this was just for tonight.

Slowly, she became aware that the music was farther away, that they'd moved on to the wide terrace overlooking the sea. He steered her around a pillar. And for the first time, she looked up at him.

His eyes were dark with an expression she'd never seen before. What was it? Desire? But that was impossible; it had been obvious from the start he could hardly stand the sight of her. Surely he wasn't interested in her in that way, was he?

"Zoe, this is exactly the reason why I've stayed away from you, why I haven't danced with you tonight. This is so not what I want, but I can't seem to help myself around you…"

Before she could ask what he was talking about, he kissed her.

His lips were warm and demanding and with a sigh she surrendered. It never even occurred to her to deny him this. To deny herself this pleasure.

Because that was what it was. Pure, unadulterated pleasure.

With a shaky exhale, she pulled him closer and thrust her fingers into his hair. He groaned while his hands restlessly explored her body. *Don't stop, please don't stop.* For a split second she worried she'd said the words out loud, but quickly remembered her mouth was otherwise engaged. As far as she was concerned, it could stay that way forever.

His lips moved from her mouth and he kissed a trail down her face, her neck, until he reached her cleavage. Breathing became impossible. His one hand cupped her curves and his tongue flicked out, following the line of her pushed-up breasts. His other hand found her bare leg under the short dress. Restlessly, his fingers caressed her leg until all her nerve endings screamed from an overload of impulses.

Her legs wobbled, and without lifting his head, he pushed her against the pillar so she'd have support. Heat spread from her belly throughout her whole body; she was going to burst into flames at any minute.

"Dale!" someone called.

"Zoe?" She heard her sister Hannah's voice from far away.

"Dale, where are you?" The voice was much closer now.

Dale's head jerked up, and breathing heavily, he pushed himself away from her.

He rushed forward towards the voice that had called him. Embarrassed, Zoe pulled at her dress. What was she thinking? Making out with Dale Cavallo of all people, where anyone, her mother included, could see her. She wasn't thinking, that was the problem. Her brain cells had ceased to function when in his arms.

She'd never kissed someone she barely knew before; she couldn't believe she'd behaved so... so sluttishly. There was no other word for it. She'd nearly had sex with a man she hardly knew and this out in the open where anyone could have seen them.

"Oh, there you are. Don and Caitlin are leaving, come on, let's go see them off," one of his brothers said.

"In a minute," Dale said.

"Where's Zoe?" Hannah asked.

"She... um... bathroom, I think," Dale managed.

And then it was quiet again. Dale walked back to her.

"We have to go," he said. "Look, I'm sorry, this—"

"Shouldn't have happened. I cannot agree more," Zoe said as briskly as she could and stepped around him.

He grabbed her hand. "That's not what I was going to say—"

"Well, that's what I'm saying. Besides, you did say you didn't want this. It was a mistake, a huge one." She walked away as quickly as she could.

Dale called out her name, but she slipped past several people and took the stairs two at a time, praying he wouldn't follow her. Her head spun, and she frantically tried to think of a way to get away without seeing Dale again. She couldn't stay there for another minute.

London. She had to be there in a week's time. Zoe

quickened her steps. This was a great reason not to travel to Cape Town tomorrow with everyone else. She'd planned to fly to London from Cape Town in a week's time anyway but leaving directly from here made more sense. Her mother wouldn't find it so strange. Susan was going to be in charge of the business for the duration of Zoe's stay in London anyway, and an extra week wouldn't be a problem for her.

All that was important now was to put as much distance between herself and Dale as possible, because she was afraid if she didn't leave quickly she might just do something extremely foolish. Like knocking on Dale's door so they could continue what they'd started minutes ago.

Her breathing was still labored. The feelings he had unleashed tonight frightened her. She had never experienced desire that strong and it was freaking her out completely. And this from a man who was so out of her league it was hysterical. What the hell was she thinking?

Dale had a very public reputation of not staying in a relationship for long. In other words, he was exactly the type of man her father was, the reason why she never let herself become too close to any man again.

DAZED, BEWILDERED, AND still reeling from the passion that had nearly consumed him minutes ago, Dale stared after Zoe. His body urged him to follow her to her room, lock the door behind them, and finish what they'd started. But the fog of his lust-induced state finally began to clear, and he was able to listen to his more rational side.

What the hell happened? He'd managed to stay away from her all night, although, as his brother had teased, his eyes had probably never left her. Not for a minute. And it would have stayed that way if her mother hadn't insisted they dance with her daughters. The minute her small hand had touched his, all the reasons he'd told himself to stay away from the woman simply vanished.

And, damn it, he'd been doing so well. But then, this afternoon, she walked down the aisle with her sisters and friend and stole away his breath, his reason, his soul. They all looked stunning, but Zoe was exquisite.

She'd done something with her hair; a long fringe, or whatever it was called, covered her forehead, and the rest was plaited and knotted into a complicated twist just behind one of her ears. The short pearl-grey dresses the bridesmaids wore were made of some or other soft material. His eyes had zoomed in to where Zoe's dress ended in a wide flare just above her knees, leaving the rest of her long legs bare.

He'd found it difficult to breathe throughout the short ceremony. But he managed to stay away from her by dancing with every other woman there. He'd nearly succeeded in leaving the wedding with his good intentions intact.

But then he danced with her. And he kissed her. She smelled like rain, tasted like no one else he'd kissed before. And now nothing else seemed to make any sense.

Chapter Three

ZOE LOOKED AROUND her office with a smile. She'd arrived back in Cape Town over the weekend and was ready to start with all the new projects Susan had been emailing her about.

The three months in London had been great, but she had missed her family and it had been so lovely to see all of them again.

And after three months, she felt confident Dale Cavallo was out of her system. Over the last few weeks she'd managed not to think of him… too often. On the steamy dreams she was still having, featuring him in every scene, she was not going to dwell.

The messages he had left for her right after the wedding to contact him she had simply ignored. At that point, she'd had no idea what to say to him. And by the time she left London to return to South Africa, she was confident she would be able to see him at family functions without changing into a stammering schoolgirl. She hadn't heard from him again; a clear indication that whatever he'd felt for a few minutes three months ago while kissing her was forgotten.

Susan knocked on her open door and entered, smiling.

"It's good to have you back after three months, Zoe. This place just hasn't been the same without you." Susan sat down on the other side of Zoe's desk.

"It's good to be back, thanks," Zoe said, pleased her thoughts had been interrupted.

"You've been away much longer that we'd hoped, but we've coped." Susan smiled, eyes twinkling.

"Yes, it took a while before Peter was completely happy. Jerry and Adam were a great help. I'm so glad they were willing to help with the project. But I think they're very glad to be back."

"Yes, that's what they said. I have to tell you, the first thought that entered my mind when you sent a message to say you're not coming back to Cape Town after your sister's wedding but leaving directly for London, was that you were eloping!"

Zoe inhaled sharply. "No!" she exclaimed before she could regain her composure. "No," she said again, trying to hide her alarm with a smile. That eloping with Dale Cavallo had actually seemed like a good idea when she'd been kissing him was not something she wanted to be reminded of, let alone share with anyone. "You know me, getting married is not on the agenda. Happy-ever-afters are not my thing."

She took the file Susan held out to her. If she couldn't even explain her frantic escape to London to herself, how could she possibly explain it to someone else? Because that was what it had been—an escape. She had fled. There, she'd admitted it. And she was very glad she left when she did.

Dale would have a new beauty in tow by now and probably didn't even remember the kiss they'd shared.

"It was just one of those things, you know? It seemed easier to fly from the Seychelles than coming back here for a week," she said vaguely and opened the file. The last thing she wanted was for anyone to know about her little… lapse. "Anyway, it's nice to be back. The project in London doesn't constantly need my attention now. I may have to return for one or more consultations, but at this point there is no reason for me to be there full time."

"I've enjoyed being in charge, but I am so glad you're back," Susan said.

"You said in your email you have several exciting projects that you've signed contracts for?"

"Yes," Susan said and leaned forward. "The one I'm most thrilled about is the contract for the Cavallos." She pulled out a contract. "I'm so pleased you've reconsidered. You have a meeting with one of the brothers later today. Dale, if I remember correctly."

Zoe froze at the mention of the Cavallo name. She stared at Susan. "What did you say?"

Susan's smiled slipped. "The Cavallos. The contract to do the interior on their hotel near the Kruger? I was under the impression you've decided you want to do it after all. They are part of your family now."

Zoe was speechless. She had given Susan the reins when she'd left for London and was happy to let her decide on which projects they would work. Susan knew the business inside out, and Zoe trusted her. It had simply never occurred to her that Dale would contact her firm for a second time. And that he'd finalize the contract without speaking to her again personally, knowing she didn't want to do it, was simply unacceptable.

"I'm sorry Susan, but I would have told you if I'd changed my mind. I told Mr. Dale Cavallo in no uncertain terms we don't want the job. Why he contacted you in my absence again I don't understand, but that's his problem. Please email or phone him and tell him we're not interested," she said with as wide a smile as she could muster.

"Not interested…" Susan said, obviously flabbergasted. "You're not serious? This is a huge job and everyone here is so excited about it. I signed the contract as was our agreement before you left, I can't now turn back and…"

"I'm sorry, Susan, but you will have to. We're not doing this job and that's final. What else is there?" she asked as pleasantly as she could.

Susan cocked her head and stared at Zoe for a few seconds. A hint of a smile turned the side of her mouth upwards, but she didn't say anything.

"What?" Zoe asked, shifting in her seat.

"Nothing." Susan picked up another contract. "I've just never seen you so upset at the mention of someone's name.

Anyway, if that's what you want, I'll talk to him. None of the other projects are as exciting, but there is a small block of offices in Claremont..."

"Good, let me look through this. I'd appreciate it if you could talk to Mr. Cavallo in the meantime and explain that we won't be able to help with their hotel."

"I'll see what I can do," Susan sang and left her office.

Only then did Zoe exhale and put her head in her hands. Of all the devious and deceitful things! How could he? She should fire Susan on the spot! Even as the thought raced through her brain, she slumped back in her chair. She had given Susan full control over incoming contracts, never thinking Dale would be so devious. He knew she'd been in London and probably knew through the family grapevine that Susan was in charge while Zoe had been away.

She quickly turned to her computer and scrolled through her sent emails. Damn it, she was sure she still had her very definite answer on an email. There it was, in writing. As she usually did, she'd also sent an email message to Dale, confirming that she was not taking the job.

And as far as she remembered, he'd accepted her answer in writing as well. She scrolled down to the email he'd sent and read through it again. He'd said he was sorry about it but accepted her decision. It was there in writing, so what happened?

There was a knock on her door and Susan entered, trying to look grave, but her eyes were twinkling just a tad too brightly for Zoe's liking.

"Zoe, I'm really sorry about this misunderstanding. You said I could sign any contract I think would suit the firm…"

"I know and you're right. But I very specifically told Dale Cavallo I don't want the job. Were you able to get hold of him?"

Susan nodded and sat down quickly. "I've spoken to him, but he said we've signed a contract and it's binding. He's expecting you this afternoon."

Zoe stared at Susan for a few minutes while frustration clawed at her insides. She did not want to work with the guy; she didn't want to see him. Seriously? Why would he insist they do this when he knew she didn't want to do it?

The kiss. Of course. He was probably looking for revenge because she had walked away before he could do so.

She finally became aware that Susan was staring at her.

Susan cleared her throat. "So, this Dale—did something happen between the two of you?"

"No… yes… no!" Zoe called out in frustration. "Nothing happened. I'll go see him and settle this. I just can't… don't want to work with family," she said, using the first excuse she could think of. "It's never a good idea."

Susan sighed dramatically. "If you say so. Everyone was so looking forward to this project and not least of all because Dale Cavallo would have been involved," she said and swooned. "He's so gorgeous. I can't believe you didn't snatch him up."

"Nobody is snatching anybody up," Zoe said, just about gnashing her teeth, and picked up one of the other contracts. "Tell me about this. It looks interesting."

With a knowing look, Susan began to talk about the project and explained some of the ideas she and the team had come up with.

Zoe tried to concentrate on what Susan was saying, but she fumed inside. The gall of the man. Except for the kiss, he'd normally just glare at her. And she was over the ridiculous crush she had on him, she was sure of that.

What had happened to change a surly Dale into a kissing one, she had no idea, but even after three months, she vividly remembered she hadn't even put up a fight. At all.

She was so ashamed of her behavior. So ashamed, in fact, she hadn't been able to bring herself to tell her sisters about the kiss, and they told one another everything.

What Hannah would say about it, Zoe could just imagine. Her sister made no secret she couldn't stand the sight of Darryn Cavallo and she kind of felt the same way about all his brothers. Don might be an exception, she actually liked her brother-in-law.

So telling Hannah had not been an option. And Caitlin was useless at the moment—she was still walking around starry-eyed and would probably think it was a good idea.

And the last person she would ever tell was her mother. Any mention of kissing thrilled her romantic soul and the scene would probably be used in her next romance novel, heaven forbid.

There was nothing else to do. She would have to meet Dale this afternoon and just pretend they'd never locked lips. Zoe touched her mouth. Oh, hell.

"What do you think?" Susan's voice penetrated Zoe's chaotic thoughts, and she pushed the contract towards Susan.

"It sounds great, thanks, Susan. I'll meet you back here later today, then you can show me what you and the team have come up with." She stood up.

Susan frowned and also stood up. "But that's what I've been doing…"

"Of course, but in more detail, I mean." Zoe checked her watch. "I… I have a few calls to make." Susan finally left.

By the time Zoe parked in front of the hotel where the Cavallos had their offices, she was a nervous wreck. She inhaled deeply, trying to get some much-needed oxygen in her lungs and lowered her head on to the steering wheel. Her breathing was erratic, her heartbeat completely out of rhythm, her hands were clammy. And all because she was going to see Dale.

Exasperated with herself and the whole situation, she flipped down the sun visor and checked her makeup in the little mirror. Her pale, worried face stared back. Lipstick. Definitely more lipstick. She rummaged around in her handbag until she found one. Good, this one was nice and red. It sent a clear I'm-in-control-and-you-are-not-going-to rattle-me message.

Finally, she got out of her car and put her sunglasses firmly in place. *He's just a man, remember?* And she'd been handling men since puberty. And whatever ridiculous feelings she'd experienced when he'd kissed her way back in February were probably the result of too much champagne. She was over the guy. Today's discussion was all business. Business that she was getting out of as quickly as possible.

Chapter Four

THERE SHE WAS. Dale relaxed for the first time in nearly three months. He was looking down from the top story of their offices in their Cape Town hotel and had a clear view of Zoe getting out of her car.

And even from this distance, desire kicked him in the gut and instantly heated his blood. He turned back to his brothers quickly.

This was one of the rare occasions when they were all in the big communal office they preferred. And although that normally meant they could settle urgent matters for a change, he wished none of them were here today. His brothers tended to stick their noses where they didn't belong.

"Zoe has arrived. I'm meeting her in the conference room," he muttered, hoping no one would notice that he was leaving. He grabbed a file and his cell phone from his desk on his way to the door.

Don got up from his desk and walked around it. "About?" he asked, and Darryn and David also looked up.

Dale sighed. Damn it, now he'd have to try and explain something he didn't understand himself. "The hotel near the

Kruger. The contract to do the interior has been signed by the woman Zoe left in charge while she was in London. This morning she phoned me, apparently wanting to back out."

David frowned. "Back up a little bit. I thought Zoe declined to work for us at the end of last year already? When did you sign this contract and how come she didn't know about it?"

"If I remember correctly, I was the one who suggested we use her and you weren't all that keen for her to do the work in the first place," Don said. "So why—"

"I'm still not keen. But I'm not going to be the bad guy here. Anyway, I've seen her firm's work in the meantime. Peter Walsh, for one, is very taken with what they've done in the London hotel. According to him, she's the best, and I thought we always use only the best."

"I still find that interesting, you know. That you got her another job when she declined the one we offered her, one far away from South Africa." Don smiled. "Any particular reason?"

"You were the one who thought we should help her," Dale said.

David cocked an eyebrow. "The fact that she is a long-legged, blue-eyed, gorgeous brunette you couldn't take your eyes off at Don's wedding has nothing to do with it?"

Dale glared at his brother. "This is business, nothing else."

"Yeah, right. I saw how you danced with her at the wedding. The two of you were practically welded together, if memory serves me right." David smiled.

Darryn grimaced. "Please, just don't tell me another one of my brothers is falling for a Sutherland. I told you to stay away from them."

With a grin, Don slapped Darryn on the back. "The way you've stayed away from Hannah? I've seen you kissing her twice now—you have a thing for a Sutherland as well?"

Darryn swore and jerked up from his chair. Dale had to end this conversation before Darryn got riled up again. It was obvious something had happened between Darryn and Hannah at some point, but it wasn't a topic his brother ever talked about.

"I don't have a thing for anyone," Dale snarled. "Zoe does interior decorating, you suggested Zoe, we need a good one, she has a pristine reputation, and her firm is well-known for delivering good work. That's it," he said, fed up at this point with his brothers. He left the room and walked towards the conference room.

THERE WAS NO logical reason why he'd contacted her firm and why he'd signed the contract without speaking to her again. There were many other reasons why he'd make sure he had a signed contract, none of them made any sense, though.

After the wedding, after the kiss, he had to stay away from her. But as soon as he heard from Don that she'd left someone else in charge of her firm in South Africa while she was in London, he'd known what he was going to do.

Getting Susan to sign the contract was easy. It wasn't as if he'd done anything illegal. He'd simply let Susan assume Zoe had changed her mind. He never actually said that in so many words though, so she couldn't accuse him of lying. Now he had a contract. One that would ensure Zoe wouldn't be able to back out, like she'd tried to do this morning.

Irrational. But then, there was nothing rational about the way she made him feel, period. For the past three months he hadn't been able to get her out of his head or his dreams, he'd missed her at the family functions and he'd realized no matter where in the world she found herself, she'd be constantly on his mind.

So his illogical solution was to get close to her, and the only way he was to do that was to get her to do work for them.

If they were to work together, if he saw her regularly, he might find all he'd been feeling was lust for a pretty face. This unrest inside of him was nothing more than having the hots for someone for a short period of time.

Any other possibility was too frightening to contemplate.

ZOE SQUARED HER shoulders and walked through the doors of the beautiful boutique hotel in Bantry Bay, one of a dozen in and around Cape Town that belonged to the Cavallos.

Like all their hotels, this one had also been designed by Dale and his signature glass exterior for most of their hotels worked particularly well here in the centre of Cape Town.

The inside of the hotel carried the same clean lines as the glass exterior. There were no upsetting patterns. Instead, the foyer was decorated in subdued greys and white. Texture had been embraced and cushions made of different materials invited guests to relax on wide couches. Big windows let in plenty of light and Zoe noticed artwork from several local artists on the walls. Grudgingly, she had to acknowledge this place succeeded in giving the feel of a home away from home.

Hurrying forward, she forced herself to concentrate on why she was here. She had to get out of this contract. Businesswise, it would be unwise though. A contract like this would be good for her firm, the Cavallo name in her portfolio would entice more clients to make use of her interior decorating skills, etcetera, etcetera.

But, darn it, it was her company and she could still decide whether she wanted a job or not. And she didn't want this job. She didn't want to work with Dale. She—

Zoe stopped in her tracks. But she was over him, wasn't she? The damn crush or whatever it had been was gone. She couldn't turn away work like this because she was afraid she would fall for a guy. That would be ridiculous.

Besides, she probably wouldn't have to work with him

personally. Surely tycoons like the Cavallos had minions running around doing most of the work. She'd do her job, take his money, and that would be that.

With a relieved smiled, she walked up to the receptionist.

"I'm here to see Dale Cavallo," she said to the smiling woman behind the counter.

"Yes, he's expecting you. Please come with me, their offices are separate from the rest of the hotel." She motioned Zoe towards the lifts.

Zoe looked around her as she followed the woman into the lift. So this was where the Cavallo brothers dreamed up plans for where their next boutique hotel would be built.

The lift doors opened on the upper floor and in front of them was a lovely room, exquisitely decorated. Here too, greys and whites were used. The whole place whispered money. Lots and lots of money. Nothing was over the top, but Zoe's experienced eye could see the curtains, chairs, paintings, and decorations were of top quality, carefully selected to create an opulent yet welcoming ambiance.

"Beautiful," she murmured.

The receptionist looked back at her and smiled. "It is, isn't it? Mr. Dale Cavallo is also a well-known architect. He draws up the plans of all the hotels and does most of the interior designs himself as well."

"Oh." Zoe couldn't manage more.

Dale also did the interior decorating himself. That particular piece of information had simply never come up in any conversation with her sister. But why, if he did the interior designing himself, would he need her firm?

"Mr. Cavallo said he'd meet you here in the conference room," the receptionist said and pointed towards an open door.

"Thanks," Zoe said and walked into the room.

She put her bag down on the first chair and took off her jacket. It was May but still warm during the day—and just thinking about seeing Dale again in a few minutes had made her hot all over.

"Hi, Zoe," Dale said right behind her and she turned around quickly.

And there he was. Deep inside her something sighed. Resigned, she acknowledged two simple facts. One, he was drop-dead gorgeous, and two, he turned her on like no one else had ever done. Was she over her silly crush? The answer was obvious.

These were the facts and there seemed to be nothing she could do about her reaction. But she didn't have to like it.

"Dale," she said as coolly as she could and pulled out the chair. "Shall we begin?"

Chapter Five

DALE PUT HIS hands in his trouser pockets. Much better to have them there. Otherwise they might just decide to do things without listening to his brain. Like touching her cheek to make sure it really was as soft as he remembered.

He took a seat at the table across from her. The width of the table should keep her scent from reaching him. She still smelled like rain. Her scent was killing him and made him want things he'd never thought of before. Suddenly, the idea of a steady relationship didn't sound so horrifying anymore. What the hell?

He opened the file. "I understood from Susan you want to cancel the contract, but—"

"No, I've actually decided that we'll do the job," she interrupted, and he looked up.

"But Susan said you don't want the job."

"I know, but I've had time to think about it and I've realized that it's a great opportunity for the firm. And I can work with just about anyone if I put my mind to it. Although, I'm curious," she said and took two pages from the file she had in front of her. She shoved them across the table to him. "There is the email I sent to you, confirming our telephone conversation and there is your answer. Your letter makes it clear that you accepted the fact that I didn't want to do the job. In fact, I know the only reason you asked me in the first place was because Don asked you to. But then, a few weeks later, you contacted Susan about it again without talking to me. Why?"

Dale leaned back in his chair and stared at her. She looked calm and very collected. Her dark hair was swept up, leaving just a few tendrils curled softly against her face. His fingers itched to touch them; he remembered the silkiness.

And then she swallowed. He bit the insides of his cheeks to prevent him from smiling. So, the lady wasn't as cool as she pretended to be.

"I tried to contact you after Don and Caitlin's wedding but you never answered any of my messages."

She narrowed her eyes. "You know perfectly well why I ignored those messages," she said primly.

He leaned forward, enjoying her obvious discomfort. "You see, that's just it. I don't know. You kissed me, stormed away, and ignored all the messages I sent you."

Her lips trembled slightly. "You were the one who kissed me," she said, her eyes stormy.

"You didn't kiss me back?" he asked, not quite under-standing why he couldn't stop baiting her.

She inhaled audibly, bent her head for a few seconds before she opened the file. "We can go ahead with the contract.

That is, if you still want me to."

"Oh, I still want you…" he said solemnly, waiting a millisecond before he added, "to."

Her flared nostrils were the only indication she'd caught his meaning.

"Good." She got up. "I'll ask Susan to contact you for the next meeting. Please make sure whoever you send has all the information available—budget, timeline, and of course, if—"

He also got up slowly. "Seeing that my brother suggested we make use of your firm, I will be working with you. Directly." He emphasized the last word. "I don't mind doing favors, but when money is involved, I have to protect the investment we'll be making. I have to make sure you're not just a pretty face but can actually do the job. You obviously don't really want to work for me, but you've realized it's good for business. Therefore, I have to make sure our business doesn't suffer because of yours."

Her eyes narrowed but met his for the first time. "You are under no obligation to work with me. Just say the word—"

"And be the bad guy in this? No way. But you'll be working closely with me."

"If that's what you want. I assumed you'd prefer I work with someone else."

He shook his head and she stopped talking. "I want you to visit the ten boutique hotels we own in and around Cape

Town. To get an idea of what I like, a feel for the kind of atmosphere we like to create in our hotels. I'll ask our secretary to arrange visits for you." He pulled out his cell phone and flicked to his calendar. "Then we can fly out to Mahé next Friday. That gives you about ten days to have a look at what we have here before we leave for the Seychelles."

ZOE STARED AT him, trying to assimilate what he'd said. "Mahé? Why do I have to fly out to Mahé? I've been to your hotel there, I've seen it, there is no need to visit it again."

While she'd been talking, he had walked around the huge table and was now standing close to her.

"Oh, but I don't agree. There is every need. You were there during a wedding. And only for two days, if I remember correctly. You will need to stay for at least a week. I'm afraid I have to insist," he said when she tried to interrupt, still smiling his I'm-a-cat-and-you're-the-mouse-I-can-play-with smile he'd been using all afternoon.

The whole conversation was ridiculous. It was now even more of a mystery why he'd insisted she do the job. He'd shamelessly confessed he was only using her firm because Don asked him to.

And she'd lost whatever advantage she thought she had when he mentioned the kiss. The obvious thing she should have done was to ignore him. But now he knew he'd rattled her. All she could do at this point was to retreat with as much dignity as was possible and to make sure the next time they met she'd be ready for him.

"I'll have to check with Susan. I've just returned from a three-month stay in London, I don't think I could leave again so soon." Without looking in his direction, she bent to pick up her handbag. When she turned around, he was standing nearly on top of her.

"Make it happen, Zoe. That's how I work. You can't do what we want if you haven't seen all the hotels. Besides, there is also a hotel on Praslin, one of the other islands of the Seychelles I would like you to see. And after that, we'll fly out to the hotel near the Kruger. It should be finished in about four months' time. Then you'll have three months to do your magic before the first guests arrive."

"Three months! You're being ridiculous—"

"And by the time we get there, we'd have agreed on exactly what I want, and I can introduce you to the suppliers, so the orders can go out."

"I'd like to use the people I normally work with—"

"Out of the question," Dale interrupted her immediately. "We use the suppliers I know."

Zoe dug her nails deep into her hands and counted silently to ten. Her head was reeling. He was talking about taking over seven months of her life. Seven months of working with him, talking to him—or rather, listening to him because he obviously didn't ever really listen himself— were going to drive her insane. A more bossy and overbearing man she had yet to meet. Add to the mess the ridiculous attraction she couldn't shake, and it was going to be a very trying time.

"Dale, why on earth do you want to use my firm if, one, you're only doing this because you feel obligated, and two, you normally do this yourself, are obviously well-organized, and know what you want?"

"Trying to back out now? I thought this was a good opportunity for you," he said.

He had moved and stood so close she could see his eyes weren't simply brown. There were golden flecks in them too, flecks which fascinated her at the moment, making it difficult to look away.

She forced herself to step past him. Damn it, what was she doing, drooling over his eyes, for crying out loud?

"Please, excuse me," she said, hoping he'd step aside to let her pass. His scent surrounded her, clouding her already befuddled brain.

"In a minute," he murmured and put his hand out.

"Dale," she whispered. Damn it, she was supposed to sound annoyed, not turned-on.

His hand froze and he dropped it. He put both hands back into his trouser pockets before he turned away.

"I'll let the secretary contact you about visits to the hotels," he said over his shoulder and left.

WHEN DALE ENTERED the huge open-space office he shared with his brothers, he was still cursing under his breath. What was it with this woman? Around her, he did irrational things. Like just now. He'd made the mistake of walking closer to her at the end of their conversation.

Up until that moment he'd felt as if he was in charge, as if he was calling the shots. She'd been flustered, and he wanted to use the advantage to make sure she'd go with him to the Seychelles.

But then things changed. Up close to her, he simply forgot to think, to breathe, to speak. He only wanted. He would never be able to look at that big table in the middle of the conference room again and not picture Zoe as he'd pictured her all afternoon—leaning back on her elbows on the dark wood with an invitation in her eyes for him.

One thing at least was perfectly clear—he was still lusting after Zoe. After three months, his desire to touch her, to cart her off to the nearest room, to make love to her until she sobbed out his name, hadn't changed one bit. On the contrary. If he wasn't mistaken, it had only intensified. And he was afraid working closely with her was not going to help him feel any differently about her.

"Meeting not to your satisfaction?" Don inquired with a smile.

"No… yes…" Dale sat down quickly and opened his computer.

"So, is that a no or a yes?" David asked.

"She's agreed to do the job because she knows it's good for business. I have to protect ours, so I'll be working directly with her. She'll have to familiarize herself with the interior of all our hotels. After I've shown her around the hotels here, we're flying to the Seychelles next Friday so that she can also visit the two hotels on Mahé and Praslin."

He started typing an email to their secretary, asking her to arrange visits for Zoe. It was a while before he realized his brothers were very quiet. When he looked up, they all stared at him.

"You're taking Zoe to the Seychelles?" Don asked. "Why?"

"I told you, I—"

Darryn swore and got up from behind his desk. "You have the hots for this woman, don't you?" he barked out. "I can't believe you're also falling for a Sutherland. I'll tell you what I've told Don, although he hasn't listened—stay away from them. They mess with your head and your... Just stay away."

Fed up with his brothers, Dale went back to his emails. "I don't have the hots for anybody, this is how I work. You've never questioned my judgment before, what the hell is wrong with you now?"

"You've never behaved crazily before," Darryn snapped.

Dale looked up again. "Oh, now I'm behaving crazily. What about last year when you and Don had me jumping through hoops to help Hannah and Zoe when Hannah had her accident on Mahé? That wasn't crazy behavior? At least we know why Don was half out of his mind, he was in love. But you? I still can't figure out what got into you."

Swearing, Darryn stormed out of the office.

Don sauntered over to Dale's desk. "You mess with Zoe, you mess with me, is that clear?" he said with a big smile, but Dale knew the tone.

"For the last time, we're going to work together. That's it. Get off my back," he growled and turned his attention to his computer. Damn it to hell. What was he doing before his brothers started interrogating him?

Chapter Six

B Y THE TIME Zoe left the hotel, her heart had finally resumed its normal pace, but she was so angry with herself for letting Dale unsettle her the way he had. She hadn't expected him to bring up the kiss, damn it. And after that, she'd been a complete mess. She hadn't been able to think straight, let alone string words together to make a coherent sentence.

"Zoe!" she heard someone call and looked up. Caitlin walked towards her all smiles and sparkling eyes.

"What a nice surprise. I didn't expect to see you here." Caitlin hugged her.

"I... um... I had a meeting with Dale," Zoe said. "You look gorgeous." She smiled and touched her sister's belly. "This little one is growing by the second." She laughed, hoping to draw Caitlin's attention away from the topic of Dale. But, of course, no such luck.

"Oh no, you don't." Caitlin pulled her to the side. "What did you have to discuss with him?"

Zoe sighed. "He... I'm going to do the interior decorating for their hotel near the Kruger Park."

Caitlin stared at her for a few minutes. "Come with me," she ordered. "We are going to have tea." She motioned towards the hotel Zoe had just left. "There is a lovely tea room with lots of decadent cake and pastries. We are going to sit down and you can tell me all about Dale."

"I don't have time—" she began, but Caitlin was already steering her back into the hotel.

"I've only seen you briefly since your return, you can spare another fifteen minutes for your pregnant sister to explain what is going on," Caitlin insisted, and before Zoe knew it, they were sitting in the tea room.

Caitlin ordered for them while Zoe looked around her. Here were the same greys and whites she'd seen throughout the hotel so far. Elegant but comfortable chairs lent a relaxed feel to the place.

"Before you try to waste time, I'm fine, baby is fine, Daddy is overprotective and driving me crazy, but we're both so excited about the little one. I'm happy. So that's my news. Now I want to know why you look upset." Caitlin smiled and sat back in her chair.

"I'm not really upset, it's just..." She didn't know how to continue.

"Yes?" Caitlin urged her.

Exasperated, Zoe flipped her hair back. "Dale wants me to do the decorating of their new hotel."

"But didn't you already tell him no last year?"

"I did. But then he contacted Susan during the time I

was in London and they've signed a contract. One I'm told I can't really get out of. Also, you know Don asked him to consider my firm, and I think he feels obligated somehow. Anyway, I've come to realize working for the Cavallos is good for business and I've agreed to do the job."

Caitlin frowned. "Then why are you upset?"

"I'm not upset—" she began, but Caitlin lifted an eyebrow.

"You're forgetting I'm your sister and I know you," Caitlin said.

She sighed. "Okay, you're right. I'm upset. He wants me to visit all their hotels, including the ones in the Seychelles."

Caitlin's eyes widened. "Really?"

Zoe nodded. "And I don't see the point. If I look at their hotels here in Cape Town, I can come up with ideas. Damn it, after only seeing this place, I can show him what I have in mind."

The waiter brought their tea, Caitlin poured and handed Zoe her cup. "I can see that leaving so soon again would be inconvenient, but it's not as if you haven't done this kind of thing before. I'm still not sure why you are upset."

"Because…" Zoe began and then just shook her head.

They drank their tea in silence for a few minutes.

"He's very attractive," Caitlin said. "They all are."

Zoe looked up quickly. "What does that have to do with anything?"

A sly smile played around Caitlin's mouth. "Just sayin'."

Zoe put her cup down. "Okay, yes, he's attractive."

"And? Has anything happened between the two of you?"

"Why would you think that?" Zoe picked up her cup again.

"Because you're blushing." Caitlin giggled.

"I'm not—" Zoe began hotly, but Caitlin giggled more. "Oh, for heaven's sake. Yes, he kissed me. On your wedding day. That's it. We both had too much to drink and... That's all."

"And why haven't you told me before? Does Hannah know?" Caitlin was obviously tickled pink about the news.

"No, I haven't told Hannah. You know how she gets when the name Cavallo is mentioned. And I was away in London... Anyway, there was nothing to tell, really. Yes, he kissed me, but he's a Cavallo, he can kiss any woman any time he wants to."

Caitlin smiled. "Ahh, now it makes sense. That kiss was the reason you decided to leave for London instead of coming home first?"

Fed up with the whole conversation, Zoe nodded.

"So, has he kissed you again?" Caitlin batted her eyelashes.

"No, he hasn't kissed me again. There will be no kissing him. Ever again."

"But you would like him to?"

Zoe gulped down the rest of her tea and got up. "Yes, I'd like Dale Cavallo to kiss me again. But then, I'd probably like a number of attractive men to kiss me. I have to go, I'll call you." She tried a smile before she turned around to leave.

But instead of making a grand exit, she saw Don and Dale standing right behind her, blocking her escape route. Between the twinkling in Don's eyes and the storm in Dale's, it was clear they had heard every word of her last comments.

She opened her mouth to say something, realized nothing she could say would get her out of this mess, so she just slipped past them and made a beeline for the front door.

ZOE STOOD IN front of the big windows in her flat. She was still so glad she had been able to buy this place in Green Point more than a year ago. It was close to Cape Town and close to the busy Waterfront, but it was far enough away that she was unaware of the daily hustle and bustle of city life. And to top it all, she had a lovely view of the Atlantic Ocean.

Her flat was in one of the older buildings that had been renovated, and she was able to get it at a fair price. The rooms were big, airy, and both bedrooms also had a sea view.

From outside she heard the low-pitched sound of Moaning Minnie, the name the locals had given the red and white lighthouse across the road because of the sound it made. It was May, the beginning of winter and misty outside tonight.

She'd had a bath and was dressed in her flannel pyjamas, her favourite. She should have been in bed already. Tomorrow was going to be a busy day. But she couldn't stop thinking about what had happened earlier.

The email she'd received from Dale's secretary by late afternoon was short and to the point. The first hotel she was supposed to visit was in Clifton, the playground of the rich and famous. Clifton was about a fifteen-minute drive from Green Point, so she didn't have to get up too early to be there on time.

She was told she'd be "met" there and she was fretting over this word. Dale had stated very clearly that he was going to work with her. Did that mean he was the one she would see tomorrow?

How on earth could she face him again after this morning? "Yes, I'd like Dale Cavallo to kiss me again," she murmured the words that had been haunting her since she had uttered them. She couldn't believe she'd told Caitlin that. And then to top it off, Dale had been standing right behind her, hearing every word.

And, of course, by this time Caitlin would have told both her mother and Hannah about the kissing and the incident. And her mother hadn't phoned her yet! Probably because she was planning an attack when Zoe would least expect it.

Aarghh. She switched off the light in the sitting room. She was going to bed.

There was a sound from her intercom near the front door. She looked at the time. It was nearly ten o'clock. Who would want to see her this time of night? She walked up to the front door and pressed the button.

"Yes?" she said in a clipped voice.

"Zoe?"

Dale? Was it Dale? Surely it couldn't be Dale? There was another buzz.

She pressed the button again. "Dale?" she asked warily.

"Yes, may I come up?" he asked.

"Why?"

"Because… just open the damn gate, Zoe. Please?"

Zoe pressed a hand to her stomach. Oh, my goodness. Dale was downstairs. He wanted to come up to her flat.

Quickly, she pressed the button to unlock the gate downstairs and stood staring at her front door. She couldn't move away. Only when he knocked on her door, did she realize she was in her flannel pyjamas and she wasn't wearing any makeup. Oh, what the hell. Let him see her like this. He would probably turn around and run. Which would be a very good thing.

Chapter Seven

S HE OPENED THE door. And there he was. Nearly two metres of drop-dead gorgeous man. How was she supposed to—

Before her befuddled brain could form another thought, he was inside her flat and had closed the door behind him. She backed up a few steps; he came closer. She tried to move again, but the wall was behind her and she stopped breathing.

Slowly, he moved closer and closer until their toes met. He put his hands on the wall on either side of her body, effectively trapping her. His face was impossible to read. He stared down at her for what felt like ages.

"So," he finally said. "You would like me to kiss you again?"

"That... that's not what I said, I said—"

"You said you'd like me to kiss you again. I was there. I heard the words."

Zoe closed her eyes so she could think. With him so close to her, it had become impossible to do. "I also said—"

He bent his head so that they were cheek to cheek, his

mouth right next to her ear. She could smell red wine on his breath. Delicious tingles swooped up and down her back.

"I don't want to hear that part again. Ever. No other man can kiss you, attractive or otherwise," he whispered in her ear.

His words robbed her of any rational thought. "Dale, please, I—" That was as far as she got.

With a groan, his lips claimed hers. She gasped, trying to get air into her oxygen-starved lungs, but his tongue dove in and joined hers. At which point breathing became unimportant, really.

Her hands landed on his upper arms, his scent filled her senses, and she was lost. Sensations raced through her body, heating her blood, sending her hormones into overdrive.

She moved closer to him and his arms folded around her, pulling her flush against his body. He was all toned muscle and, where their bodies met, hard as a rock.

Unsteady fingers released her ponytail from the elastic that was holding it in place and combed through her hair.

Muttering, he buried his face in her hair. "You smell like rain. No one else smells like this, just you," he whispered before he claimed her mouth again.

His words inflamed her overstimulated senses further, and she lifted herself on her toes so she could curl her arms around his neck. She didn't want this to ever end.

Hands swept down her side, awakening every nerve ending in their wake. How was it possible to be twenty-seven and never to have experienced so much emotion in so short a span of time?

Somewhere in the recesses of her mind, her brain was trying to be heard, was trying to tell her to push him away, but her body wasn't paying any attention. Instead, it was begging to be touched, to be caressed. He obviously knew what he was doing, and her whole being was lapping up every sensual stroke.

Restlessly, his hands moved beneath her top and he touched her naked flesh. The sensation of his hands on her inflamed skin buckled her knees and he pressed her back against the wall without lifting his mouth from hers. He parted her legs with his one knee and pressed his leg against her heat. Her pulse went into overdrive.

He lifted his head and looked down at her. His breath was erratic, his eyes molten liquid. She shivered.

Slowly, he unbuttoned her flannel jacket, never taking his eyes from hers. Talking, thinking, breathing became impossible. She could only feel—the heat of his fingers where they brushed against her skin, his unsteady breath against her face, his muscled upper arm rippling under her fingers.

By the time he'd finished, she'd forgotten her own name. He moved the panels of the jacket to the side, put his hands again on either side of her head on the wall, and stared down at her for endless minutes. Although he didn't touch her, her body reacted to his heated gaze, her nipples hardened, her breasts felt heavy as if he were already touching them.

"You're so, so beautiful," he whispered and bent down to kiss her mouth again while his hands remained on the wall behind her.

Frustration clawed at her insides. Why didn't he touch her, why didn't he take her to bed, make love to her… But then slowly reason intruded through the fog of need. She had to work with him, for him, she shouldn't be kissing him, let alone be standing nearly naked in front of him. What was she thinking?

"Dale." She tried to speak but his lips wouldn't let hers go.

FROM FAR AWAY, Dale heard Zoe's voice, but he was so focused on kissing her, he didn't want to listen. He shouldn't have come here tonight. He shouldn't be kissing her, shouldn't have opened her jacket because now he'd seen her, touched the velvet texture of her skin, and he didn't think he would ever be able to forget it.

He couldn't remember the last time he'd been so hard for a woman. All he could think of was getting as close to her as was humanly possible, to bury himself so deep inside of her they would become one. Because he was afraid that was the only way he would be able to still this desperate need that was wreaking havoc inside of him.

Her hands pushed against his upper body and, gasping,

he lifted his head.

"Dale, we can't do this," she whispered shakily and closed the panels of her pyjama top.

He still had her trapped between his arms and for one wild moment he wanted to ignore her words, wanted to pick her up and take her to bed.

But his sanity returned, and not a minute too soon. What the hell was he doing? With a curse, he turned and moved away from her.

"Dale," she said again and put a hand on his shoulder.

"Don't." He growled without looking at her. "If you touch me now, I won't be able to stop."

"Oh," she said, dropped her hand, and her voice caught in her throat.

"Bathroom?" he asked through gritted teeth.

He should talk to her but needed some distance first.

"First—" She cleared her throat and tried again. "First door to your right," she said.

He nodded and walked towards the door. He needed a moment to get himself under control. But inside the neat little bathroom, he realized this was so not the right place for that to happen. Her scent lingered in the air, making it impossible to breathe. And to make matters worse, a selection of tiny, black satin and lace panties was hanging on a line above the bath.

Damn it. Now he knew exactly what she wore under her clothes. The woman was driving him insane and she didn't even know it. Swearing, without consciously deciding what he was going to do, he plucked one of the panties off the line and pushed it inside his trouser pocket. He leaned on the washbasin with his hands, willing his body to behave.

But the panties in his pocket were like a living, breathing Zoe stuck to his body.

Swearing again, he opened the door and stormed out. She was standing in the kitchen, her hands still holding her pyjama top in place.

"This shouldn't have happened," she said, her face expressionless. "We have to work together and—"

"You're right," he interrupted and rubbed his face. "I know," he said and walked past her to the front door.

He opened the door and turned back.

"If you're worried that this will change my mind to use your firm for the job, you can relax," he said cynically.

She'd followed him and was standing just behind him, her head held high, her hands still trying to keep her jacket in place.

"That is not what this is about, and you know it," she said softly. "You also know this shouldn't have happened."

While she was talking, the one side of her jacket slipped, leaving the top part of her creamy breast visible.

And that was all that was needed for desire to race through his blood again.

He put out his hand and touched her face. "You're right," he said solemnly. "But I don't have to like it." He looked down as his hand folded around her near-naked breast. On her indrawn breath, he flicked the beaded nipple with his thumb before he dropped his hand.

"Oh," she whispered, and her mouth fell open.

Swearing, he bent down and gave her a soft kiss. "Don't look at me like that," he muttered and kissed her again.

Her hands pushed against him and he lifted his head.

"Now look what you've done." He groaned and looked down. Without her hands holding the jacket in place, there was nothing keeping it from falling open.

"You did this!" she called out in frustration and grabbed the sides of her jacket. "Just go, please?" She hissed and glared at him.

"I'm going, but I've taken a keepsake," he said and pulled the panties partly from his pocket.

He hadn't intended to tell her, but he wanted to leave her feeling as unsettled as he was at the moment. Damn it, he didn't have to be the only one suffering.

And on her indrawn breath, he grinned and left. "Lock the door," he called over his shoulder.

FURIOUS WITH DALE, but mostly with herself, Zoe locked her front door and buttoned up her pyjama top. What was she thinking kissing Dale Cavallo like that, letting him touch her the way he had?

Muttering and cursing, she switched off the lights and

stormed to her bedroom. She wasn't thinking, of course. Around him, thinking became difficult, impossible, really.

Pacing up and down in her bedroom, she replayed every minute of the time he'd been in her flat. He'd probably had one glass of wine too many. That was perhaps his excuse. But she'd had none. Absolutely none. She'd been stone-cold sober. She should have ordered him to leave, not given in wantonly to his first caress.

She closed her eyes, her body vividly remembering every stroke of his hands. Oh, hell, this was not helping. He had taken her panties, put them in his pocket, and left with them. And desire was back, stirring her blood, heating her body until she found it difficult to breathe. She should be outraged, indignant, not turned-on, damn it!

She jumped up. He was a Cavallo, one of the richest men around. She should remember that. To him, she was just another woman in a long line of conquests. There was no way he could be seriously interested in her. Why on earth he'd come here tonight was beyond her. He was from such a different world, why would he waste time on someone like her? Keeping the help happy?

Finish this job as soon as possible—that was what she should keep reminding herself. And that meant she had work to do. There was no way she was going to sleep anyway, and some ideas for the interior for the Cavallos' hotel had been swirling around in her head. That was of course for the few milliseconds she hadn't been thinking about Dale.

Maybe if she could come up with something that could wow him, she wouldn't have to go to the Seychelles with him.

Because she knew—going to an exotic island with Dale Cavallo would be a very bad idea.

Chapter Eight

WHERE THE HELL was she? Dale stopped pacing and for the umpteenth time looked at his watch. His secretary had assured him that she'd sent Zoe an email, giving her the time and address of this hotel.

And okay, it was only a few minutes past ten, but why wasn't Zoe on time?

He was in a foul mood and having to wait for the woman responsible for that was not improving his disposition. Sleep had evaded him most of the previous night and he placed the blame squarely on her shoulders. And the damn black panties...

Swearing, he tried to breathe normally. What made him go to her place last night he didn't want to dwell on too much. *Blame the wine, blame her telling her sister she'd like to kiss him again, blame the fact that she also mentioned kissing other men.* He didn't even know her yet, but just the thought of other men putting their hands on her had him grinding his teeth. So, like a caveman, he had to somehow stake his claim.

This situation was fast becoming out of control. He

couldn't do his work, he couldn't even get excited about cycling—the one thing that normally helped him to relax. And to top it all, he hadn't even looked at another woman since he'd seen Zoe for the first time. She was taking over his life and he didn't like it one bit.

She was doing this job because it was good for her firm, he shouldn't forget that. He closed his eyes and remembered the silkiness of her skin, the heat of her mouth. Damn it to hell. He rubbed his face. He didn't do relationships, he kept forgetting that.

Relationship. That word again. Damn it, he didn't want a relationship with anyone, least of all with a woman who seemed to be able to turn him inside out even when she was kilometres away.

The mess with Tammy confirmed what he'd believed— women could fake interest in him if they wanted something badly enough. And they always seemed to want something.

True relationships where respect and love played a role were rare. Yes, his parents had been married for forever and it was obvious they still adored one another. But he didn't know anyone else who'd stayed married to the same person for long.

Don's marriage obviously didn't count at this point. He was completely smitten at the moment, but then he'd only been married for a few months.

Although Caitlin was beautiful, Dale couldn't help wondering whether Don wouldn't at some point fall for one of the many gorgeous women they met on a regular basis.

Thinking about Zoe this often over such a long period of time was plain scary. Somehow he'd have to distance himself from her. Hell, he didn't even have to work with her. There were other employees who normally consulted with outside contractors, and that was exactly what she was—an outside contractor. One who'd taken on a job she didn't want to do in the first place because she knew it would further her career. She had even been upfront about her reasons. Maybe if he started thinking of her as pure business, his body wouldn't keep taking over his brain.

He felt her presence before he saw her. And he smelled her before he turned around. And then he forgot to breathe. She was dressed in neat charcoal pants, a frilly kind of white blouse neatly tucked into the waistband, and over it she wore a light pink jacket. Her hair was neatly twisted and pinned up, leaving her long neck bare. Sunglasses hid her eyes. A laptop case was slung over her one shoulder, a handbag over the other.

It was a very neat outfit for work, but if she was hoping to look businesslike, she was not succeeding. She looked sexy as hell. All he could think of was taking down her hair and getting her naked. He knew exactly how soft her skin felt, how neatly her breast fit into his hand.

He wanted to tell her he had a room upstairs with a huge bed covered in black satin sheets where they could spend the rest of the day. He wanted to describe to her in detail what he wanted to do to her, with her.

"You're late," he snarled instead.

This was business, damn it. After this meeting he was going to get on his bike and cycle until he'd be too tired to think about having sex with this woman.

And then he was going to phone one of the very willing women listed in his little black book. Hell, he didn't have to spend his nights taking cold showers. He was thirty-one, not fifteen, for crying out loud.

She pressed her lips together and nodded.

"The traffic—" she began, but he turned his back on her and started towards the lift.

"You know traffic is bad, you should've left earlier." He growled and pressed the button.

ZOE INHALED SLOWLY while she followed Dale into the lift. The doors closed silently and the two of them were alone while they travelled upwards.

It was clear Dale was in a bad mood and she wasn't going to dignify his last comment with an answer. Lack of sleep had left her feeling grumpy, and she was using all her control to try and behave civilly. Add to that the ridiculous effect the man had on her and she shouldn't talk about anything else but work today.

She had promised herself she would behave like the professional she was supposed to be and not let him affect her again like he'd done last night.

Although they were both facing the doors, she was aware of everything about him—his scent, his breathing, the heat of his body. And she recalled every stroke of his hand over her skin the previous evening.

Just when she thought she was going to do something foolish, the lift stopped and the doors opened.

"This way," Dale said in a clipped voice and pointed towards a big room opposite them.

He waited for her to step out and, as they walked towards the office, he put his hand to her back. She had to swallow the sudden lump in her throat. She loved seeing a man touching a woman like this, loved seeing how he instinctively tried to protect the woman he was with even though she didn't need it.

"I have the plans for the hotel near the Kruger Park here," Dale said and walked towards a big table in the middle of the office. "I thought we could start by looking at them first. The layout is slightly different to what we've done so far. Then, afterwards, I'll show you around this hotel. If you have time, I would also like to show you the one near the Kirstenbosch Botanical Garden today."

He bent over the plans that were spread out on the table. "You can see on this plan that the hotel has been built around a big marula tree. We didn't want to chop that down and it also brings the bush closer to the guests, we argued."

"I remember seeing it, yes," Zoe murmured and looked

to where Dale's tanned hand was pointing.

She tried to focus on the plans and not his hand, but it was such a struggle, and after a few minutes, she gave up.

"Can I take these with me?" she asked and put out a hand to pick them up.

"Certainly not." Dale growled and quickly folded the plans. "If you want to look at them, we look at them together. I don't trust anyone with my work."

Confused, Zoe stared at him. "But how am I supposed to—"

"If you want to look at the plans, you come to me."

This, she'd never had to deal with before. She'd try something else.

"Do you have something specific in mind?" she asked, trying her best to sound cool and collected. She touched her laptop. "Because I have some ideas I could—"

"Not before you've seen all the hotels," he interrupted her. "I thought I made that clear. You can put your laptop back in your car."

He turned to leave the room and for one moment Zoe considered sticking her tongue out. But she bit her lip and followed him. There was a contract; this was going to be good for her business. Maybe if she kept repeating these words, she might be able to concentrate on what she was supposed to do.

"AND THIS IS one of the bedrooms…" Dale said and opened the door.

Zoe entered the lovely room, trying not to look at the huge bed. Hopefully she could leave after this. They had spent most of the morning looking around in the first hotel before setting off for this one opposite the botanical gardens. She had insisted on driving herself here and couldn't wait to leave.

Like the hotel she'd been in yesterday, this one also had glass all around, but it was a much smaller, more intimate hotel than the big one in the city. The interior reflected what she'd now come to realize was Dale's preference—understated, quiet, with a splash of colour here and there.

Her shoulder muscles were stiff from trying to keep herself together. She hadn't eaten this morning, had refused tea when he'd offered it earlier and now her blood sugar was low, her hormones driving her crazy, and she just wanted to go home.

"You'll see—" Dale said again but his phone rang. He looked at the number and his face lit up. "Just a sec." He turned his back on her.

Zoe walked towards the bathroom but could hear every word of Dale's side of the conversation.

"Cybil, darling!" he gushed. "I've just been thinking about you this morning," he said in his velvety voice.

Zoe walked into the spa-like bathroom but could still hear what Dale was saying. It was obvious he was talking to a woman and equally obvious he was very happy to hear from her.

"Tomorrow night? That sounds great. I'll pick you up at seven?"

He finish the conversation and she walked back into the room, making notes and trying to ignore the sharp pain that had lodged itself close to her heart.

Irritated with herself and with him, she put her notebook back in her handbag. "I have to leave," she said. "Thanks for showing me around. But surely you have enough to do and don't have time for this? I could even visit the rest of the hotels on my own. I know now what you want me to look at."

He lifted an eyebrow. "You've agreed to my terms, nothing changes that," he said coolly.

"Fine," she said and walked past him as quickly as she could. "According to the schedule I got from your secretary, we're going to your hotel in Stellenbosch tomorrow, I'll meet you there," she said without stopping.

"I'll pick you up—"

"No, thank you. I'll meet you there," she said and before he could say another word, she walked out of the door.

SHE WAS HUNGRY, tired, and upset. She took the stairs, not wanting to be cooped up again in such a close space with Dale.

Her phone rang. It was Hannah.

"Are you free tomorrow night?" Hannah asked.

"Yes, I am," Zoe said fervently. "Where?"

"Sea Point?"

"La Perla?"

"Seven?"

"Yes!" Zoe called out, smiling for the first time today.

"I'll pick you up," Hannah sang and rang off.

Zoe pulled the pins out of her hair, shook it loose, and got into her car. At least she had something nice to look forward to.

WHEN DALE REACHED the window of the room he'd just shown Zoe and looked down to the parking lot, he was just in time to see her hair tumbling down over her shoulders. A need so fierce that it robbed him of his breath seared through his body.

She had her phone to her ear and was smiling.

Something he hadn't seen her doing today.

He turned away. Tomorrow night he was taking out another woman and he was going to enjoy every second. He was going to have sex with her as soon as was decently possible because, damn it, he had to get Zoe Sutherland out of his system.

The only reason she'd agreed to do this job was because it would be good for her business. She was like all the other women he'd met—not really interested in him as a person but more in what he had and what they could get through him.

At least she didn't pretend to like his company; today she'd been all business and cool. The way he'd wanted it, the way he'd made sure it stayed all day.

So why the hell did he keep thinking about her wrapped around him, her body pressed close to him, her lips underneath his? Damn it, he had to get laid tomorrow night or he might do something he'd regret.

At least he'd left the damn panties at home this morning. Not that it was helping. He could still picture her wearing them.

Swearing, he stormed down the chairs. His phone rang. It was Darryn.

"Yes," he answered shortly.

"I have a date tomorrow night," Darryn said grumpily.

"So have I," Dale said and couldn't help smiling at his brother's tone. "But at least I don't sound so unhappy about it."

"Join us, please? I'll pick you up."

Dale frowned. Darryn sounded weird. "Is everything okay?" he asked.

"I'm fine. Just want everyone off my back for a change, Mom especially. I'm taking a woman on a date. Are you joining us or not?" Darryn asked irritably.

Dale just laughed. Normally Darryn was a nice guy, but

over the last few months, he'd been impossible to have around. Maybe spending time with him after work was a good idea.

Chapter Nine

I T WAS A beautiful autumn day. There wouldn't be many more of these gentle days. According to the newspaper, the first cold front was making its way towards Cape Town. That normally meant winds, storms, and rain.

Zoe parked behind the hotel. The setting of the place was ideal, right in the heart of the town. She didn't see Dale's car. It would seem he was the one who was late today. She'd left Cape Town early to make sure she would be on time and already had a cup of coffee in one of the many coffee shops Stellenbosch had to offer.

Her phone rang. It was her mother. Zoe was wondering when she'd phone. Caitlin would have told her about their talk at the Cavallo hotel already.

"Hi, Mom," she said and held her breath.

"Zoe, sweetheart, I'm still trying to catch my breath! I've heard that you've kissed that delectable young man!" her mother gushed. "Good for you."

Zoe smiled. Her mother was incorrigible. She was over sixty but always talked in exclamation marks. And when the subject was kissing, she was over the moon.

"It really was just a one-time thing, Mom," she said, crossing her fingers. There was no way she was going to tell her mother about the second round of kissing. "How are you doing?"

"I'm fine, my dear. As always. But you're not going to get me sidetracked. I want to know every last detail."

Zoe got out of the car. "I have a meeting, Mom. I'll phone you later this week, okay? But there really isn't anything to tell."

It was quiet for a few seconds.

"Oh, come on, Zoe, I'm your mother. Tell me something, I'm looking for inspiration for my new book."

Zoe giggled. "Oh, Mom, you're hopeless. What do you want me to say?"

"Well, how was it? Just a quick touching of the lips? Were tongues involved? Did you like it?"

"Mother!" Zoe called out, flushing. A good thing her mother couldn't see her now. "I'm not going to tell you that!"

"Oh, all right," her mother grumbled. "I'll use my imagination on the specifics. But on a scale from one to ten, how would you rate his effort?"

Zoe was silent for a moment. "You only have a ten-point scale?" she teased.

Her mother inhaled audibly. "That good?" she whispered in awe.

"That good."

Her mother sighed. "Oh, lovely. Just lovely. Okay, sweetie, I have to go and work," she said hurriedly and rang off.

Grinning, Zoe grabbed her tablet and bag and walked towards the hotel. The tablet is easier to use than her laptop when walking around all day. Her mother was happy. She was going to write about kissing.

Zoe fanned herself. Just talking about kissing Dale had her all flustered. She inhaled the fresh air and tried to calm down. Stellenbosch was only about an hour's drive from Cape Town.

It was a beautiful and busy student town. The town was well-known for its huge oak trees, some of which had been planted in 1683 by the Dutch East India Company governor of the time, Simon van der Stel. Fortunately, those in charge had managed to save some of the historical buildings that had been standing there since the founding of the town. She didn't often get a chance to visit but had always loved the vibe of the town.

Zoe looked up at the hotel as she approached it and couldn't help an appreciative sigh. She had wondered whether this hotel would also have a glass exterior like the others. Situated here, she'd thought the modern glass look Dale preferred would look out of place. But he'd somehow succeeded in combining glass with the typical Dutch-styled houses one could still find around the town.

She stepped inside the hotel and couldn't help another

sigh, this one of relief. There wasn't any sign of Dale yet. She took a seat on one of the couches and looked around her. The inside of the hotel had the same understated elegance she'd seen in the others. Here white had been combined with beiges in different textures and shades.

She found herself fidgeting and willed her shoulders to relax. Just the thought that Dale would be there any minute had her restless, unsure of herself, and she hated to feel like that. Why would she be this way around him?

Yes, he was attractive and sexy as sin—all the Cavallo men were. Why then was it only when she was with him that her hormones went haywire? And how could she understand his behavior?

Two nights ago, he'd turned up at her flat, told her he didn't want her kissing other men. He'd kissed her, had her just about naked in front of him, took her panties with him, and yesterday she could've been chopped liver for all the attention he gave her.

At the thought of the panties he'd taken, her face suffused with heat and her heart started doing cartwheels. She should give her mother that tidbit at some point—she would love to use it in one of her stories.

This—whatever it was going on between her and Dale—was also just make-believe, it wasn't real. As she knew all too well, in the real world men didn't stay around forever, not like in her mother's stories where the heroine always got to marry the hero. She had to stop dreaming and thinking about this guy.

It wasn't that she didn't like men. She enjoyed their company, she'd even had sex on two occasions. Experiences that had left her frustrated and disappointed. She'd probably expected something of the fireworks her mother always wrote about in her romances but, as she should have known, those were fairy tales, not real.

She'd definitely never met anyone who'd led her to believe in the happily-ever-afters her mother described.

And it wasn't as if Zoe's home life had been a good example of marital bliss. Yet, her parents seemed to be quite happy being divorced. Her mother had a very full life; her dad always had a different woman on his arm.

Okay, Caitlin seemed to be quite happy at the moment. But what was going to happen once the baby was born and Don had to leave for business? Would he still be faithful? Would she be happy staying home?

Relationships were just so complicated and, from what she'd seen so far, they mostly ended where one or both parties were angry or hurting. And, anyway, with a father like hers, she was plain wary of men.

It would be much better to remain professional when Dale was around. She was going to tell him about her ideas for the hotel this morning. Hopefully, he'd give her a chance to at least explain what she had in mind. And that would mean they wouldn't have to spend quite so much time together.

She frowned. Somehow, she would have to get hold of the plans of the hotel, though. How Dale thought she could work without them, she had no idea. And there was no way she was going to contact him every time she wanted to check something on the plan. She'd ask again nicely and if he still refused, she'd have to make another arrangement.

She felt him behind her before he spoke.

Shaking her head at her own foolishness, she got up.

"Dale." She nodded in his direction without looking at him.

"Zoe," he said, sounding businesslike.

Good. Now if she could only keep this up for the rest of the visit.

DALE QUICKLY TURNED away from Zoe and looked around for the manager. If he didn't talk to someone else quickly, he might just do something crazy like taking Zoe to one of the suites in the hotel and locking the door behind them.

Today she was wearing a tan jacket over a coral-coloured dress that ended demurely just above her knees. But the flesh-coloured high heels she wore showed off her gorgeous legs, and all he could think about was gliding his hands up and up—

"Mr. Cavallo, sir."

Dale looked around gratefully. The manager was approaching from behind him.

"Henry." Dale greeted him and introduced Zoe without looking at her.

How the hell was he going to keep his hands to himself? By insisting on being with Zoe when she visited the hotels, he was punishing himself. As if it wasn't enough that her damn black panties had him dreaming X-rated dreams for the last few nights. Also his own bloody fault.

He could get someone else to show her around. Hell, he should get someone to show her around. Maybe he should excuse himself and let Henry take her around.

Before he could say anything though, Henry opened the door to one of the bedrooms, and Zoe smiled at him before entering. Henry's gaze dropped to Zoe's legs. A primitive need to guard what was his welled up inside of Dale.

"Thank you, Henry, I'll take it from here," he said brusquely and followed Zoe into the room. There was no bloody way he'd let the fool follow Zoe around, drooling over her legs.

Zoe was standing in the middle of the large bedroom, looking around her. All Dale could see was the big bed and all he could think about was having Zoe on it, under him, above him, all over him.

Cursing softly, he turned away from her and walked to the big doors that opened onto a courtyard.

"This hotel is similar to the one near the Kruger in that it's also built around a courtyard, although of course here there is no marula tree. But like the new hotel, all the bedrooms open up onto the patio," he said and walked out of the room. Staying close to that bed was not a good idea.

"Dale," Zoe said behind him and he turned around.

"I think I have a good idea of what you like and I've made some notes of what could be done. We could save a lot of time if you are willing to look at what I've come up with so far. You must be busy and must have other projects to work on as well."

Dale looked at her for a moment, enjoying her beauty, her poise, her grace. Hell, she was exquisite. His fingers tingled. She was right. Before he did something he'd regret, they should try and finish this.

"We have an office here, follow me," he said curtly and turned away quickly.

ZOE FOLLOWED HIM, her eyes taking in everything from his broad shoulders to his very sexy behind. By the time they stopped in front of what looked like the office he'd mentioned, she was just about salivating.

Dale showed her to a chair near a big desk and she opened her tablet. He walked around and sat on the other side of the desk. Thank goodness, at least she could breathe again.

"From what I've seen so far, the interior of your hotels convey a kind of elegance, a sense of classiness without being austere—is that also the kind of feel you'd like in the new hotel?"

Dale frowned. "Yes and no. The hotel is situated in the bush. I'd like people to be aware of where they are, but of course in luxury."

Zoe nodded and opened the icon on her tablet to show Dale her ideas. She pushed it towards him.

"I'd like to create a romantic mood—"

"In the bush, really?" Dale chipped in sarcastically.

Zoe counted silently to ten and continued as if he hadn't interrupted her. "That will contrast with the ruggedness of the environment. I was thinking white and khaki with a dash of something playful thrown in like a bold red."

DALE LIFTED HIS head quickly. That was exactly what he'd had in mind. Exactly. But she didn't have to know that so soon. That they were thinking along such similar lines was freaking him out a bit. He tried to relax and leaned back in his chair.

"How did you come up with that idea?" he asked mildly.

"I keep ideas in a file and when I looked through some of the clippings, that was the one that caught my eye," she said and pointed to the picture on the tablet.

"What about an African theme—a completely rugged and African look?" he asked innocently.

Clearly stunned, Zoe stared at him for a few seconds. "You can't be serious!" she called out. "It's been done to death and, frankly, if that's what you want, I'm not the person for the job." She reached out to take her tablet.

Dale put a hand out at the same time to pick up the tablet and their fingers touched. Both froze. Zoe's eyes flew up to his. He was momentarily taken aback at what he thought he saw in them—confusion laced with something else. Was it desire? Before he could decide, she'd lowered her eyes and taken the tablet.

Dale stood up. She stopped talking. And looked up at him.

"Do a complete proposal and let me have it when you're ready," he said. Stick to business. Stick to business. He should keep repeating this mantra until he actually complied with it.

Zoe stood up as well. "Could I have a copy of the plans, please?" she asked. "It would be very difficult to do a complete proposal without the actual plans in my hand."

Dale shook his head vehemently. "I told you. If you need to see the plans, you ask me."

"Dale, surely you can see that—" She faltered. He'd been moving closer while she'd been talking. She folded her arms in front of her.

"That I need those plans and—"

He only stopped when he was standing right in front of her. With only his finger, he touched her mouth.

"We all need something, don't we?" he asked. "But we rarely get what we want."

For long minutes they stood like that, their breaths mingling, his finger on her face.

Zoe stepped back.

"Dale, seriously? You know as well as I do that it's impossible to work without the actual plans."

"You can come and work in our offices, but you won't get a copy."

"But that's ridiculous!"

He shrugged.

Zoe spun on her heel and stalked towards the door. Just before she walked out, she turned back. "If you're happy with the proposal, do I still have to go to Mahé?"

"You can only finish your proposal once you've seen the two hotels on Mahé and Praslin as well. So, yes, you still have to go."

She didn't answer. She only turned and left him without another word.

IRRITATED WITH HIMSELF, Dale stared after Zoe as she walked down the corridor. Damn, she was sexy. Cursing, he turned away and realized he was smiling. Damn it to hell, why was he smiling?

For her, this was just business. He should remember that. She kept asking about the plans after all. But his body wasn't listening to his brain. That was why he couldn't stop thinking about her in the big bed they'd seen this morning, or on the table in the conference room where they sat yesterday, or on any damn surface, for that matter. He just had to see her, to want her.

This madness had to end right here. The problem was that he'd been without sex for three months and tonight that was going to change.

He had a date. Not with Zoe Sutherland. With another woman. And he was looking forward to it. Cursing, he walked around his desk. And he was going to keep telling himself that until it was true.

Chapter Ten

"SO, CAITLIN AND Mom say you've kissed Dale Cavallo," Hannah said.

Zoe nearly choked on the sip of champagne she'd just taken. The waiter had just moved away.

"It was nothing." She coughed and dabbed her lips with the serviette, hoping to buy a little time before answering.

Hannah angled her head. "I can see that," she said drily and sipped her champagne.

"Seriously, I told Caitlin it was a combination of too much wine and a lovely evening. We're… we're family, for heaven's sake," Zoe said. "I was hoping I'd see more of you while I was in London, but you only managed one visit."

She held her breath, hoping Hannah would change the subject.

"Nope, not going to work. You are not getting me off this subject so quickly," Hannah said and leaned forward. "I also hear, to my surprise I might add, that you are going to Mahé with Dale."

Zoe sighed. Clearly Hannah was not going to leave the subject of the Cavallos alone.

"Hannah, really. I'm going to Mahé to work. Dale wants me to look at the hotel there and also to visit the one on Praslin. That's all. What is it with you and the Cavallos anyway?" she asked, irritated. "You snarl the minute their name comes up in a conversation."

"Let's just say I've had a bad experience with one of them and I don't trust them around my sisters." Hannah frowned.

"What happened?" Zoe asked.

Hannah stared into her glass for a moment before she threw back her head and downed the rest of the champagne. "On the plus side—I'll also be in the Seychelles around the time you'll be there."

"That's wonderful!" Zoe called out, grateful the topic had been changed. "Are you there for a shoot?"

"Yes, probably only for three days, but I'll let you know. We usually stay in the Cavallo hotel on Mahé, so I'll be able to see you in the evenings. The days will be too busy." Hannah smiled.

"That's really great news. I haven't received the final arrangements, but I can't think that we have to be there for more than a few days either," Zoe said. "It's so nice to know you'll be around. You can show me the hot spots of the island one evening."

"That's a date. The weather should be nice, you should take your bikini and work on your tan—you're much too pale after your stay in London."

"I know—the London weather was terrible. But I was

kept so busy, I didn't really have time to worry about it."

"Who were the people you worked for?" Hannah asked. "I don't think you ever mentioned their names."

"I worked with Peter Walsh and never met the owners—"

Hannah inhaled quickly.

"What?" Zoe asked.

"Peter Walsh? The last time I heard that name, he was working for the Cavallos."

Zoe stared at Hannah, her head reeling. "But... why didn't he say anything? Why didn't any of the Cavallos mention the fact that I'd be working for them?" Zoe asked, now getting angry.

"Maybe he's not working for them any longer." Hannah shrugged. "Does it matter?"

"I... don't suppose so. But why not tell me? I—"

"Hi, Hannah, I didn't know you were back."

Surprised, Hannah looked up at two attractive men who'd approached their table. "Hi, Steve, it's so nice to see you."

Steve introduced his friend Paul and Hannah introduced Zoe. They spoke for a few minutes, until Steve, obviously reluctant, touched Hannah's shoulder.

"I wish we could join you, but we're entertaining clients and have to go; they're probably wondering what happened to their hosts," Steve said.

Paul took Zoe's hand and kissed it. "I would have loved to stay as well." He smiled before taking a step back.

"Of course, nice of you to stop by." Hannah nodded with a smile.

"Steve looks like a nice guy," Zoe said when the men had left. "And he was kinda drooling over you." She giggled.

Hannah shrugged. "He's nice enough. And I've done ads for his company, but…" She shrugged again.

"There's no spark?" Zoe asked.

"Not even a flicker."

Zoe threw up her hands. "Why is that? Some guys are so nice, they'll make good husbands, will look after you for the rest of your life, but there is no attraction. And then there are those—"

"Who turn you on even when they're not around; make your knees weak even though you know there can be no future with them?" Hannah finished her sentence.

"Exactly." She nodded then frowned. "But then I look at our father and it seems he finds a spark whenever he meets a woman."

"Which means there must be other men out there that we'll find attractive." Hannah smiled.

"I really hope so," Zoe said fervently before taking another sip of her champagne. Then, smiling slyly, she leaned back. "Who is the man who is currently weakening your knees?"

"I didn't say there is one—" she started, but Zoe shook her head.

"You said, other men we'll find attractive, which implies

there is one you find attractive at the moment," Zoe insisted.

"And you said you really hope so, which also implies that there is someone you find attractive at the moment." Hannah laughed.

But then Hannah's gaze moved past Zoe. Her face froze and her smile disappeared. She quickly looked down at her glass.

"Talk of the devil," she muttered.

"What's wrong?" Zoe asked and put her glass down.

"It's the—"

"Good evening, ladies. I didn't know you were back, Hannah."

Zoe's heart dropped and she glanced up. Dale and Darryn stood next to their table, two blondes hanging on to their arms for dear life. A sharp pain just below her heart made it difficult to breathe.

"Darryn," Hannah said and picked up her menu.

Zoe just nodded in Dale's direction. She couldn't meet his eyes, didn't want to look at the woman on his arm, didn't want to see how someone else was clinging to him. She also picked up her menu.

It was quiet for a few moments.

"Can we find our table, Darryn, darling?" the woman next to him whined.

"Enjoy your evening," Dale said, and thankfully they all moved away.

Hannah signaled to the waiter.

"I'm in the mood for pasta, what do you think?" she asked with an overly bright smile.

"Great idea. Any dish, you pick," Zoe said and put the menu down. The neatly typed letters just didn't make any sense at the moment.

While Hannah placed their order, Zoe tried to calm down. Damn it, she hadn't even looked at the man properly and her whole body was on fire. Irritated with herself, she fidgeted with her cutlery. That she could react to him this way, in spite of the fact he had another woman on his arm with whom he was probably spending an entire evening, was downright humiliating. He clearly had no trouble forgetting that he'd kissed her a few nights ago.

Hannah leaned back in her chair. "Who's going to say it?"

"Say what?" Zoe asked, even though she knew exactly what her sister was talking about.

"Who the men are we were talking about just now?"

Zoe sighed. "Okay. Dale is… attractive and I… he…"

"Turns you on?" Hannah smiled cynically.

"Yes," Zoe hissed, shaking her head at her own silliness. "And for you it's Darryn?"

"Oh, yeah." Hannah grimaced. "But mostly I succeed in ignoring it. Nothing will come of it. Ever. And, please, we never had this conversation, okay?"

"Okay," Zoe readily agreed. "Let's talk about something else. I'm hoping we could fit in some serious shopping before we leave for a tropical island, don't you agree?"

Hannah seemed as eager to change the topic as Zoe was. The waiter brought their food and they talked about everyday things until they finished their meal.

"Would you like anything else?" Hannah asked.

"Thanks, no. I can't eat another bite. Let's have coffee at my place," she said, and Hannah nodded while signaling for the waiter to bring their bill.

The waiter smiled and came closer. "No bill, ladies. Your bill has been taken care of."

"But..." both she and Hannah began, but a smooth voice interrupted them.

"There's no way I could let two beauties like you pay for your own dinner," Steve said as he approached their table. "My treat, please. I only hope next time I will also have the pleasure of your company." He helped Hannah out of her chair.

"Thanks, Steve." Hannah smiled and kissed him on his cheek.

"Yes, thanks." Zoe smiled and started getting up. But before she could move, Steve's friend Paul was there, holding out a hand to her.

"Thanks, guys," Hannah smiled.

Zoe smiled up to Paul. "Thanks," she said. He was quite attractive. Surely she could feel something for any other attractive man?

The men escorted them to the front door of the restaurant and waved as they left.

"Steve really is a sweet guy," Hannah muttered and grabbed Zoe's hand before they crossed the street.

"So is Paul." Zoe smiled. "Maybe we should agree to go out with them. You never know, some kind of spark just might develop."

Hannah opened the car door. "Let me know how it works for you," she said drily. "I've tried dating other men and haven't had any luck."

Zoe stared at her sister. She was very much afraid that she would come to the same conclusion. And then she was angry. Damn it, she was all tied up in knots because he'd kissed her, and he blithely moved on to the next woman. Men!

Chapter Eleven

DALE WAS TRYING to look intrigued by what Cybil was saying, really trying. But he was losing the battle fast. This had been such a bad idea. The woman was beautiful and sexy but boring him out of his mind. All he'd been thinking about the whole damn evening was the woman who sat across from them at another table. Zoe.

It was so crazy that they'd picked the same restaurant the sisters did. It was not as if there weren't any other nice places around. In this part of town there were too many to count. But he and Darryn had agreed quickly that this was where they wanted to go to.

After this morning, he had tried to put Zoe out of his mind and focus on his date for the evening. But his body wasn't interested in anything his brain was trying to convey.

And to make matters worse, he had to witness another man touching her. He didn't like that. At all. He had another woman with him, there was nothing between him and Zoe, and the fact that another man touched her shouldn't bother him. Except, it did.

When he and Darryn had entered the restaurant earlier

with their dates, he'd known Zoe was around even before he'd seen her. Something happened to the air around her, something he picked up on every time.

So when he turned around and saw her there, laughing with her sister, he wasn't even surprised. His first ridiculous reaction was to be relieved. Relieved because she was with her sister and not with another man.

And, hell, she looked magnificent. She wore a tight-fitting, short grey dress, seemingly demure, but he caught a glimpse of a pair of high-heeled sexy black boots peeping out from underneath the table. His heart lurched, his pulse quickened, and both had yet to settle down.

Zoe's cool gaze when Darryn stopped at their table infuriated him. She'd barely glanced in his direction. And all he could think of was kissing her until the coolness disappeared. Because he'd felt the heat beneath her cool façade, knew exactly what to do to bring it to the surface.

He'd also seen the whole exchange between the two sisters, the waiter and the two men who had just about been slobbering all over them. He'd seen it because he had been watching Zoe for most of the evening. And what he realized now was that if he couldn't come up with an excuse why he and Darryn had to leave quickly, Dale might just do something extremely foolish.

"Are you ready to leave?" Darryn asked in a clipped voice, and before anyone could answer, he signaled to the waiter to bring the bill.

Relieved, Dale stood up. Darryn was clearly also not enjoying his date. "I'll settle the bill, you get the car," Dale said and left. Behind him he could hear the two women asking Darryn what was next on the agenda for the evening.

He turned back to offer an excuse for why he had to go home, but Darryn was already talking to them.

"Maybe another night, ladies, we have an urgent early morning meeting," he said.

Dale settled the bill and went out to find his brother. Usually an evening with Cybil ended in bed, but tonight he couldn't wait to drop off his date. Just the idea of touching someone else was making him feel ill.

At least one thing had become quite clear this evening. No other woman would do while Zoe Sutherland occupied his mind, body, and soul.

SOMEHOW, ZOE WASN'T even surprised when she heard the buzzer of the door downstairs.

She pressed the button. "Dale?" she asked in as cool a voice as she could.

"Zoe... how... Yes, it's me. May I come up?"

Zoe's finger hovered for a second before she pressed the button to open the gate downstairs. Then she opened the front door and walked back to the lounge. Hannah had had a quick cup of coffee, but had left a while ago, thank goodness. She didn't want to think about what her sister would have said.

She sank down on the couch and combed back her hair. Damn it, she should be in bed, sleeping, but she was so restless and kept thinking about Dale—about the woman on his arm, about why she was upset to see him with someone else, about Peter Walsh working for them, about how and why she got the job in London.

At least now that Dale was here he could provide answers about Peter Walsh. It was the only reason she was glad he was coming up the stairs to her flat.

The front door closed.

"Zoe?" Dale called, and she heard him walking down the corridor.

"Come in, I'm here," she said at the same time as he appeared in the doorway.

Her heart lurched, the way it always did when she saw him. Damn it.

She attacked, flinging out questions before she said something she'd regret. "Why didn't you tell me Peter Walsh worked for you? And whose idea was it that I got work in London? And why?"

Without saying a word, Dale lifted an eyebrow and slowly advanced until he stood in front of her. She had to bend her head backwards to look up at him.

For long minutes he stared down at her until her neck protested.

"For heaven's sake, sit down," she said, irritated.

He took the seat next to her on the couch.

"What are you going on about?" he asked mildly.

She turned to him, realizing too late that now she was nearly sitting on top of him. "I… what…" she stammered, and he smiled.

Fed up with him, with herself, and the whole situation, she took a deep breath. "Peter Walsh, does he work for you?" she asked.

"Yes, he does."

Zoe frowned. "Whose idea was it to offer me the job in London?"

"Mine."

Exasperated, Zoe stared at Dale. He didn't even look worried or ashamed or guilty.

"Why?" she demanded. "At the time I told you I didn't want to work with you, why did you get me a job in London?"

"I didn't get it for you. You were merely offered the job. You could have turned it down," he said as if it was the most logical thing in the world.

"Dale, why didn't you tell me? Why did you do that? I don't understand. What—"

And then he kissed her.

HE HADN'T PLANNED the kiss. But that was the only way he could think of to stop her from asking so many damn questions. Hell, he didn't know why he did anything when she was around—why he was here, why he'd dropped off a very beautiful and willing woman without even so much as kissing her, why all he could think of was to get here. To be here. With Zoe. Trying to explain something he didn't understand himself was impossible.

Her lips opened in a surprise gasp, and he pulled her closer, his tongue seeking entrance to the wet depths of her mouth. He swallowed the groan from deep within her throat and teased her tongue with his.

"This is such a bad idea," she murmured against his lips but didn't pull away.

"I know," he agreed huskily and intensified the kiss. Right now, he didn't want to talk, to think, because what was happening between him and Zoe was way beyond anything that could be discussed, dissected, or understood. It just was.

The velvety texture of her skin egged him on to explore what he knew to be underneath the tight-fitting dress she wore. Restlessly, his hands molded her body to his while he searched for the zipper at the back of her dress. He slowly began to lower it.

"Dale." She gasped and lifted her head.

His hand on the zipper froze. Passion had darkened the blue of her eyes. She put a hand out and touched his mouth.

"What is this?" she whispered, frowning. "This... thing between us? I don't even like you."

He combed back her hair, noticed his fingers were unsteady. He tried to smile, but he didn't think it was working.

"I... don't know. All I know is that I want you with a need I don't understand. There is nothing logical about this—hell, you're not even my type. You're too... distracting." He grimaced, and she lifted an eyebrow and tried to move back. But he held on tightly. "But I want you. That is all I know now."

Her gaze roamed over his face and he groaned. "You're not helping if you look at me like that." He growled and kissed her.

He lifted his head a fraction. "At this point I can still walk away, but I don't know about five seconds from now."

ZOE TRIED TO rationalize the situation, but her usually neat and orderly brain had stopped working altogether. He wanted her, and for once in her life, she was not going to overthink a situation.

She went with her instincts. "I don't want you to go," she said and got up.

She bent her hand backwards and slowly pulled down the zipper of her dress. Dale's eyes never left hers.

"Let me," he said, his eyes glowing, and he got up. His warm hands folded over her shoulders and he turned her around. It was becoming increasingly difficult to breathe. He lifted her hair, and his lips warmed against her neck while his other hand pulled the zipper all the way down.

Slowly he pushed her straps over her shoulders until her dress dropped to the ground. All she was left wearing was a matching set of bra and panties in red lace and her boots.

Groaning, he turned her around, his eyes dark pools of molten liquid. Without taking his eyes from hers, he stroked his hands up and down her sides. "Beautiful," he whispered. "Just beautiful."

His words banished the last of her doubts and she took his hand. Even if she could be with him for only this one night, she didn't want any regrets. "The bedroom is this way." She smiled and led him down the short corridor to her bed.

As IF IN a trance, Dale followed Zoe all the way to her room, his eyes fixed on her very sexy bottom in the red, lacy panties and on the black high-heeled boots she was wearing. He remembered the black silk number he'd taken from her bathroom, the cause of his X-rated dreams since then. After tonight, he'd probably never be able to fall asleep again. By the time she turned around, he was hard and throbbing with need for her.

She lay down on the bed propped up on her elbows and lifted one leg. Dale feasted his eyes on her body while he slowly pulled down the zipper of her boot. His hand trailed behind, discovering every contour, every toned muscle of her long legs. Her breath caught in her throat, but she swallowed and lifted her other leg.

When he was done, his hands stroked the silkiness of her long limbs almost reverently, and with every touch, he teetered closer and closer to the edge of an unknown abyss. He was burning up. Swearing under his breath, he quickly got rid of his clothes. Just before he threw his pants down, he remembered to grab a packet out of his wallet. She smiled until her eyes dropped down to see the very obvious sign of his need for her.

The smile wavered and with big eyes she looked up at him.

This time he smiled. "Like what you see?" he teased and knelt down beside her.

"Oh, yeah." She breathed and invited him closer with her arms.

"Relax," he whispered. "This is for you."

He pinned her hands above her head and took his time looking over every centimetre of her body.

Bending down, his mouth began an exploration of her skin.

ZOE COULDN'T STAY still. She wiggled her arms free and brought her hands down so she could touch him. Her body moved closer to his, begging for his touch, wanting to experience more intensely what his mouth was doing to her.

Sensation after sensation raced through her body, leaving her quivering and out of breath. Her senses were totally focused on the man touching her—his scent, the nonsense he was whispering against her skin, the steel of his muscles under her fingers.

His fingers followed his mouth and lace and satin disappeared in between their sighs.

"You are so beautiful." he crooned again, and at that moment she felt treasured, loved, special.

Going with her instincts, she lifted herself and nudged him over so he was lying down and she could glide over every hard muscle of his firm body.

"I believe in taking turns," she whispered.

He grunted, but she ignored him. She bent down and while her hands explored his muscled torso, her lips began their own discovery and tasted and savored his hot flesh. His unique scent weaved around her and pulled her further into a vortex of feelings and emotions she hadn't known was possible up till now.

Her hand moved lower; his breath became labored. When her hand found him, he groaned.

"You like that?"

"Oh, yeah," he whispered as her fingers caressed him.

INTENSE WAVES OF desires threatened to choke him. Cussing, he pulled her up.

"Don't." he growled, and before she could blink, she was lying on her back.

"I'm so hard for you, if you keep touching me like that, this will be over way too soon," he whispered and slid his hands over her body.

Dale was struggling to form a coherent word, let alone speak a complete sentence. There was a roaring in his ears making it difficult to think of anything else. The only thing that mattered at the moment was pleasing this woman.

He found her core—she was wet and ready for him. A tenderness he hadn't experienced before washed over him. He wasn't quite sure what was happening to him, but for the first time his own needs weren't that important.

"You're ready for me," he whispered and trailed his damp fingers over her body.

"Please, I..." she pleaded until his fingers found her again.

"What?" he teased and kissed her. "Is this what you want?" He found her nub again.

"Dale!" His name fell from her lips, her body bowed towards his and he couldn't wait another second to make her his.

He quickly sheathed himself and moved over her. "Look at me," he urged and wonder spread over her face as he entered her.

ZOE TRIED TO keep her eyes open, tried to watch Dale's face as they became one, but powerful emotions were sending her into a spin and she gave up the struggle and closed her eyes. Sensation after sensation gushed through her being and left her stunned. Surely no one person could experience something so intense and survive?

But there was more. Dale drove into her once again, and she was lifted even higher. With his name on her lips, she hovered for long minutes above a steep cliff before she tumbled down, down, and down until finally spent, she could float in calmer waters.

Chapter Twelve

WHEN DALE OPENED his eyes, she wasn't there. The change in the air around him when she was near had gone. His first reaction was one of relief. He had no idea what to say to Zoe this morning.

He'd never experienced anything so all-consuming as their lovemaking the previous night. He felt confused, wrung out, mangled, exhilarated, and completely freaked-out. What she could do to him with just a touch of her hand scared the hell out of him.

He got out of bed and glanced back at the tangled sheets. And became hard again just thinking about the warm, willing woman he'd had in this very bed throughout the night. They probably hadn't slept for more than an hour. Every time she'd turned, he'd woken up, hard for her. And every time she'd been ready and eager for him.

Pulling on his pants, he walked towards the kitchen. The smell of freshly made coffee hung in the air. On the counter he found a tray with a mug, milk, sugar, and a fresh croissant. The rest of the place was neat as a pin. There was a note on the tray.

For minutes he stared at the tray, trying to put a name to what he was feeling. Up till now the only woman who'd ever made coffee for him in the morning was his mother. He never stayed around during the morning-afters with women; he was always the one to leave. This time the woman had walked out on him, though. But had made him coffee. And had left him something to eat.

He poured coffee into the mug, took the note, and walked towards the big windows facing the ocean. The sky was overcast and the sea looked grey and gloomy.

He looked down at the note in his hand and skimmed through the few words...

Dear Dale. Like we've agreed—this was a bad idea. I'm flying out to Mahé today. I've spoken to your secretary, she's organizing everything. I'll contact you when I'm back. Zoe. P.S. The door will lock automatically when you close it.

Swearing, he walked back to the couch, sat down, read through the note again. He leaned back, finished his coffee while staring out over the sea. Well, hell. The last sentence of the message got stuck in his mind. *The door will lock automatically when you close it.*

Was that true for everything else as well? Or did it just work with her front door?

A strange pain lodged itself inside of him and he rubbed over his chest, trying to ease it.

This was actually a good thing. He should be pleased. He thought he'd have to do his usual explanation of hey-remember-no-strings-this-was-just-a-casual thing, yada-yada-yada. But now, no excuse was necessary. It would seem the lady had the same idea. What felt like a hole opened up inside of him.

So this was it. He stood up, washed the mug, cleaned the coffee machine, walked back to the room, stripped the bed, put the bedding in the washing machine, had a shower, dressed himself and left her flat, closing the door behind him as she'd instructed. By then, the hole inside of him was as big as the wide-open spaces of the Karoo. He tried not to think about the fact this would probably be the last time he'd be in Zoe's flat.

As he waited for the door to lock behind him, the lift doors opened. For a second his pulse quickened, but it was Hannah who stepped out. Her eyebrows rose when she saw him.

"What are you doing here?" she asked coolly. "Where is Zoe?"

"I've spent the night," he said deliberately. "And according to a note your sister left me, she's on her way to Mahé."

Hannah's eyes narrowed. "What did you do to her?"

FOR THE FIRST time since opening his eyes, he smiled. "A gentleman never tells."

For a moment, he thought she was going to take a swing at him. But she got back into the lift, muttering furiously under her breath.

"I've warned her about you Cavallo men, I told her you will hurt her. But would she listen? Oh, no, she—"

The lift doors closed on a fuming Hannah. Dale stared at the door. What had Zoe told Hannah about him that had led her to warn Zoe he'd hurt her? Or had Hannah's warning more to do with Darryn than with him? The two of them always seemed to be at odds with one another.

Not bothering to wait for the lift, he walked slowly down the stairs while he tried to process his thoughts. He tried to be honest with himself.

He'd come here last night because he didn't like the fact that another man had touched her. He'd come here because he'd wanted her. And they had sex. Sex? Was that all it had been? Damn it, he didn't want to think about it!

And why had she made coffee for him, left him something to eat, if being with him had been such a bad idea?

Hurt and irritated with himself, he left the building and walked across the parking area to his car. Damn it, the woman had left. They'd spent a night together. That was it. Which meant she was now out of his system, like he'd wanted. There was no reason for him to follow her to Mahé. If he was honest, the only reason he wanted her to go with him in the first place was because he wanted her back in that exotic location to take up where they'd stopped the last time they'd been there. When Don and Caitlin had gotten married. He'd wanted her in bed.

BUT NOW THAT he'd had her, he could carry on with his life. He'd see Zoe when she got back, would leave her to finish the job and that would be that.

There was no need to spend another minute thinking about the woman.

He drove away from Zoe's flat, images from their love-making last night replaying in his mind's eye over and over again. Swearing loudly and furiously, he stepped on the pedal.

How the hell was he going to forget about her?

HANNAH PHONED AS Zoe boarded the plane.

"What happened between you and Dale Cavallo?" Hannah hissed before Zoe could even say hello. "I told you not to get involved with him."

She swallowed. "I can't talk now, Hannah, I've decided to leave for Mahé earlier. We're about to take off."

"Dale told me. I'll also be in Mahé tonight, I got an earlier flight."

Zoe sighed. "Fine, see you later."

When the plane finally took off, Zoe relaxed and berated herself. She'd been worried Dale would follow her but realized now how ridiculous she'd been to think that. To him, she was just another conquest.

Before she'd forced herself out of bed this morning, she'd stared at him for long minutes. She'd wanted to stay so desperately, but she knew what would happen. He was going to scuttle away as soon as he could without looking her in the eye and she didn't want to see that. Why would he want to stay? He was a Cavallo, for crying out loud; there was no way Dale would've wanted to repeat the previous night. He'd had his way with her. Now she'd be out of his system.

And what about her? Well, if she was quite honest, she'd been hoping for the same thing. But unfortunately she was now afraid one night with Dale Cavallo was never going to be enough. She was very much afraid there was no easy way to get him out of her system.

She tried to inhale, but her body felt too small all of a sudden. Being with him had been a magically, intensely beautiful experience, one she would never forget.

But she lived in the real world and what she was feeling, what she'd experienced last night, couldn't be real. She was just another woman in a long line of women he'd had. There was no way he'd be interested in repeating the experience. She closed her eyes and didn't bother to brush away the tears that rolled down her cheeks. If he were, he would have been at the airport.

DAVID BROKE THE silence in the office.

"So, what's wrong with the two of you?" he asked and pointed towards Dale and Darryn. "I thought you had a hot double date, but you've both been snarling and barking at everyone since early this morning. What happened?"

"Mind your own damn business," Darryn growled.

Before Dale could say anything, the door to their office flew open and Caitlin stormed in.

"You and you," she said very quietly, pointing at Dale and Darryn. "What have you done to my sisters?"

Don appeared behind her, his eyes blazing.

"What did you do to upset my wife?" he barked.

"What are you talking about?" Darryn asked, his face closed.

"Zoe left for Mahé this morning early and Hannah is also on a flight heading for the Seychelles. A week before they were supposed to go. The only reason could be the two of you. So, I repeat, what have you done to them?"

"I—" Dale began, but Darryn interrupted.

"Dale and I had dates with two other women," he said mildly. "So the erratic behavior of your sisters is not our doing."

Caitlin stared at Darryn, her eyes mere slits.

She turned to Dale. "Do you have anything to add?"

"No, ma'am," he said. This was clearly not the time to tell her he'd ended up in bed with her sister.

Caitlin pointed a finger at both of them. "The last time

Hannah was in Mahé, she ended up in the hospital. We still don't know what really happened, but I know she was scared of something. If anything happens to my sisters, and I mean anything, I'm holding the two of you responsible," she hissed, and turning on her heels, left the office.

"Well?" Don said. "Anything?"

Dale got up and grabbed his laptop. He was not going to get any work done in this chaos.

"I'll be working at home," he said and left before Don could say another word. Dale had had enough of inquisitive, meddlesome brothers for one day.

But Caitlin's words left him restless and, yes, worried. He'd forgotten about the incident where Hannah had been hurt. All he remembered was his brothers' crazy behavior. At the time, he hadn't really paid much attention to what had really happened to Hannah. It was news to him that she'd been scared.

Hit and run? Yeah, that was what was said, anyway. Someone had nearly run her over, but the car had raced away quickly and was never found. He wondered whether there had been a proper inquiry into the incident.

He would phone the hotel tonight and make sure the sisters would be escorted if they ventured out. It wasn't necessary for him to fly out to Mahé. Zoe knew what to look for in the hotels. His secretary had told him she'd arranged everything, but would she be all right?

Oh, why the hell was he still thinking about Zoe?

Chapter Thirteen

ZOE STOOD IN the foyer of the hotel. She was waiting for Hannah. They'd managed to have a quick breakfast together this morning. Her sister had promised to show Zoe the nightlife on Mahé tonight, and she couldn't wait to get out of her room. All that she'd been thinking about since she'd arrived had of course been Dale. And what had happened between them the last time she was in this hotel.

Zoe rolled her shoulders to try and relax. Why she was so tense, she had no idea. The flight from Cape Town the previous day hadn't been that long, about seven hours. And because she'd been flying business class, it was actually a very pleasant experience. Normally, she'd be crammed up in economy class with the rest of the working world, but apparently the Cavallos did things differently.

Before she left, she'd also phoned to ask for a digital copy of the plans of the hotel. Dale's secretary was out, but the person who answered the phone promised to find out where it was and would email it. She really needed it to get a complete picture of the hotel. According to the contract Dale had signed with Susan, her firm would be responsible for everything—from planning the interior decorating, to getting suppliers, right up to furnishing the hotel. How he figured she'd be able to do that without the plans, she had no idea.

She wanted to use the time she was here to finalize her proposal. The sooner she could start working on her own, the sooner she could finish and could go on with her life. The one where Dale Cavallo wasn't getting her hormones into a tizzy every other second.

Part of the day she'd been resting and the other part she spent looking over the hotel. The setting was, of course, stunning. From the top stories she could see a three-hundred-and-sixty-degree view of the ocean.

And although she'd never willingly admit it to Dale, the interior was just perfect for a hotel on an exotic island.

Classy. That was the one word that described all the hotels she'd seen so far. There was nothing ostentatious, in-your-face, about the interiors of the different hotels, but the understated elegance invited, tempted, enticed, excited. As she had come to expect, neutral colours were used, and the big comfortable couches were covered in different hues and different textures of the same colour. Dale obviously knew what he was doing. Which raised the question again—why had he insisted that she become involved?

At least she was really enjoying this trip. It was giving her a chance to get the much-needed distance from Dale, and she could look at his hotels without his constant hovering.

This morning she'd been taken to Praslin, the other big island that was part of the Seychelles and had visited the Cavallo hotel there. The ten kilometre by nearly four kilometre island was beautiful, and she'd spent about two hours touring the whole place.

It was easy to see why the Cavallos had decided to build another hotel there—Praslin seemed to provide a base for excursions to the neighbouring islands, some of which were important sanctuaries nurturing rare species of endemic flora and fauna.

And she'd fallen in love with the island's pristine beaches, especially the one called Anse Lazio, which was on the northwestern side. It was apparently rated as one of the ten top beaches worldwide.

She could see herself spending long, lazy days simply lying on that beach, and spending long, lazy nights making love to… No, damn it, she was not going to go there.

"Hi."

She heard Hannah's voice and turned around gratefully. She didn't want to spend another minute thinking of what-ifs with Dale.

She and Hannah burst out laughing. They were wearing very similar outfits, something that happened often. Tonight, they were both wearing grey pants with blue tops.

"We've done it again." Zoe beamed. "I'm so glad to see a familiar face." She hugged her sister. "So, where to?"

Hannah grabbed her elbow and pulled her towards the

big doors of the hotel. "I thought we could walk, it's such a lovely evening and—" Hannah stopped suddenly, her way was blocked by one of the hotel staff.

The big man bowed in their direction. "Ms. Sutherland, Ms. Sutherland. We are here to escort you—"

"Thank you, but that's not necessary." Hannah smiled. "We are going to the little place just around the corner."

He didn't budge. "That's fine. But we'll escort you."

"Look, it's not that we don't appreciate it, but—"

"We have no choice," he said. "Mr. Darryn Cavallo insists and—" he began to explain, but Hannah inhaled sharply and held up her hand.

"It's fine. We'll eat here."

She turned and walked towards the restaurant in the hotel. Irritated, Zoe followed her.

"Why would Darryn have us escorted?" she asked. "And why are we listening to someone who isn't even here?"

"Oh, who knows why Darryn Cavallo does anything," Hannah muttered as they entered the restaurant. "Let's eat here. The food is best on the island anyway, and the night is young."

"Table for two," she asked at the counter. She gave their name and the maître d' smiled broadly. "Of course, you are to be our guests anytime you want to eat here."

Hannah was about to erupt and Zoe grabbed her hand.

"Please follow me," the maître d' said and led them to a table overlooking the sea.

"Thank you," Zoe said. "This is lovely."

Hannah sat down, clearly angry. "The bloody man," she hissed the minute the maître d' left. "He's always rude when I'm around, but ever since the car accident last year, he's forever keeping tabs on me. It's driving me insane!"

"Really?" Zoe asked. "I didn't know that. Why…"

Hannah grabbed a menu. "Like I said, I don't know."

"Well, it's nice that they want to pay for dinner," Zoe said soothingly. "After all, we are family."

"It's okay for you. You're working for them. But I pay my own way while I'm here. At least until the shoot begins. Then obviously the client will pay.

"But my staying here doesn't have anything to do with Darryn. He makes me so mad. Ever since the accident—" she began but shook her head.

"What really happened?" Zoe asked. "We've never talked about it. I was in London at the time and only heard that you were in hospital after the fact."

"It's nothing. Darryn made such a huge thing out of it, but I was fine."

"Do you think that's the reason why he wants us to be escorted around?"

Hannah sighed. "Darryn and I—" She shrugged and smiled. "I don't want to talk about him anymore. Let's pretend our evening has just started."

Zoe looked at Hannah a moment longer. There was something her sister was not telling her. Hannah had always been the more private one and didn't share as easily as she and Caitlin did. If something was wrong though, or if something bothered her enough, she'd talk about it in her own time.

"Fine by me. Let's start with a nice bottle of bubbly, agreed?" She smiled and signaled for a waiter.

Hannah nodded and her eyes twinkled. "And if they want to pay for our meal, let them pay. We can't help it if we have expensive tastes, can we?" she said and ordered one of the more expensive bottles of champagne on the menu.

"Hannah, no." Zoe giggled. "We can't."

"Oh, yes. We can," Hannah said. "That will hopefully teach him not to have us followed around and not to insist on paying for everything."

"It's just a pity that we can't go out in the evenings. I'd have loved to see more of the island at night." Zoe sighed.

"Who says we can't go out?" Hannah asked and lifted an eyebrow. "Told you the night is young. We'll have a meal, wait until no one is looking and then go out to enjoy the nightlife." She smiled. "There's a bar in this same Beau Vallon part of Mahé and it's open tonight. Just give the protectors Darryn has appointed a chance to relax." She glanced in the direction of the two security guards. "We say good night, tell them we're having an early night and when their backs are turned, we slip out."

Zoe giggled. "You think it can work? Won't they be at the front doors?"

Hannah grinned. "There are other doors. For instance, if you go through the kitchen …"

"Sounds as if you've done it before?"

Hannah sobered. "I always make sure about all the exits." She didn't elaborate but immediately changed the subject.

Something was going on in Hannah's life that she didn't want to talk about. From past experience, Zoe knew it wouldn't help to keep asking Hannah. When she was ready, she'd tell them what was bothering her.

"YOU'RE SURE YOU'RE not twins?" the one guy asked for the umpteenth time.

Zoe laughed and shook her head. "No, we're sisters."

She and Hannah had managed to give the security guards the slip by pretending to go back to their rooms. But they stopped the lift on the second floor, took the stairs down and slipped out through the kitchen from where they walked to the nearby bar.

The two cameramen had joined them a while ago. Apparently, Hannah knew them well. Both were charming and attentive. Really nice. But, even though she'd really tried, there was absolutely no spark. Only one man could turn her on.

Smiling, she tilted her head to wink at Hannah because she was sure her sister was thinking the same thing. But Hannah's head was turned away and she was looking over her shoulder.

When Hannah looked to the front again, her smile was gone. She jumped up. "Thanks guys, but we have to go," she said and tried a nervous smile.

Zoe quickly got to her feet. Something was wrong. "You okay?"

"I'm fine," Hannah said but glanced over her shoulder again while she fumbled with her purse. She took out several notes and threw them on the table. "Our share, thanks guys!" She grabbed Zoe's hand.

"Hannah, what's wrong?" Zoe asked, stunned at the transformation in her sister.

Minutes ago she'd been relaxed, laughing, enjoying the evening. Now she was pale and clearly nervous. Something must have spooked her.

"We have to get back to the hotel as soon as possible. I'll explain when we get there."

The place was packed, new customers were still entering, and they struggled to keep together as they moved towards the entrance. Someone shoved from behind, and Zoe got separated from Hannah.

"I'll wait for you outside," she called out to Hannah, who just nodded while she kept glancing around her.

Zoe pushed through the people until she was finally outside on the sidewalk. She looked behind her for Hannah but couldn't see her sister. She walked backwards, lifting herself on her toes to see where Hannah was.

Finally she saw Hannah's face in the crowd and she waved. Hannah, clearly relieved, began moving in her direction. Zoe turned around, looking for a place where she could wait for her sister.

She bumped into someone and turned to apologize, but before she could complete her movement, there was a hand on her back that gave her a forceful push. Gasping, arms flailing, she was propelled forward and fell on her hands and knees among the milling crowd of people. She tried to get up, but someone pushed her again so that she fell on to her side. Then, from behind her, someone gave her a vicious kick and she cried out.

For the first time, people noticed what had happened and moved to form a circle around her. Hannah came barging through the circle and knelt next to Zoe, tears running down her cheeks.

"I'm fine." Zoe winced and sat up. "I'd just like to know who the idiot was who pushed and kicked me—"

Hannah inhaled sharply and glanced around them. "Can you stand up? We have to get to the hotel as soon as possible." She pulled at Zoe to help her up.

"Out of the way, please," someone with a loud voice ordered the crowd, and the security guard from the hotel and two others stepped through the line.

"How did you know where we were?" Hannah asked.

"Mr. Cavallo told us to make certain you're safe at all times. We followed you here," the guy said solemnly. "I saw that you didn't go to your rooms but left through the kitchen."

They helped Zoe up and, flanking both her and her sister, moved quickly towards a vehicle that was parked on the sidewalk.

As they drove the one block towards the hotel, reaction set in and Zoe started shivering. Her hands and knees were burning from the fall, and she was deeply sore where the kick had landed.

Hannah folded her arms around her. "I'm so, so sorry. I should have known, but I didn't expect—It was because you were with me that you were harmed." She sniffled and held on tightly.

"Hannah, what on earth are you going on about?" Zoe asked and pulled out of her sister's arms.

Hannah wiped her cheeks. "What happened back there? That was no accident, Zoe. You were mistaken for me. I thought I saw him. That's why you were shoved and kicked. He thought it was me."

"He? Who are we talking about? What—" But the car had stopped in front of the hotel and their doors were opened. As Zoe climbed out of the car, someone pushed a wheelchair closer.

She shook her head. "I'm fine. Really. I can walk—" But they ignored her and helped her into the wheelchair.

Hannah came closer and picked up Zoe's hands to inspect them. "Look at your hands," she whispered and sniffled. "Where else are you hurt?"

"I was kicked," Zoe said and touched her back. "Ouch," she exclaimed as a spasm of pain hit her.

Hannah sniffled, hugging her gently. "They're going to take you to your room and a doctor will have a look at you," she said gently. "I'm going to have a word with the security people."

"What is going on, Hannah?" Zoe asked anxiously. Obviously something was very wrong.

"It's a long story. I'm just so sorry you had to be caught up in the mess. Let me try and sort this out, then I'll talk to all of you."

Zoe hugged her, felt her sister trembling. "I'll come with you, I'm really fine."

But Hannah moved away, shaking her head. "Let a doctor have a look, please? I'll come when I'm done here."

As she was wheeled into the hotel, Zoe closed her eyes. What on earth was going on in Hannah's life? She was seriously worried about her sister.

Ouch, her hands and knees were burning fiercely now, the pain at her back was throbbing, and she felt like crying. She wished Dale were here. As the thought popped into her head, she blinked and opened her eyes wide. Dale had his fling with her. It was over. Somehow she had to learn to accept that.

Chapter Fourteen

DALE WAS PACING. He'd tried to do some work but gave up after a while, realizing he wasn't getting anything done. Then he tried the gym, and although he was beat after his workout, his brain still refused to settle down.

He couldn't put a word to what he was feeling, but something was just off. He kept thinking about Zoe. And that wasn't something new, he seemed to be always thinking about her. But he was on edge, unsettled, and these were not familiar feelings.

The manager at the hotel on Mahé had assured him they'd make sure the two sisters wouldn't go out alone and mentioned that Darryn had left similar instructions. Still, he just couldn't settle down.

Maybe he should fly out to Mahé tonight. They'd just bought a small plane for the company, because relying on the usual modes of transport was getting in the way of business. Their plane was at Cape Town International Airport at the moment, and as far as he knew, none of his other brothers had indicated they'd be using it.

He made up his mind quickly. Staying here meant he

was not going to get anything done. That had become very clear. Something inside of him was urging him to fly out to Zoe, and he'd always relied on his instinct.

While he looked around for his cell phone, it rang. The hotel in Mahé. Something cold touched his insides and he knew. His gut hadn't been wrong. He quickly answered.

The security guy spoke in a clipped voice. "I'm sorry Mr. Cavallo, but there has been an incident."

Dale sat down, the sudden roaring in his ears making it nearly impossible to catch what the guy was saying.

Minutes later, they'd finished speaking, and Dale sat staring at his phone, trying to make sense of what he'd heard.

His phone rang again. It was Darryn.

"You heard?"

"Yes. Look, I'm going to fly out there tonight. I was going to anyway…"

"Why? It sounds as if she's fine," Darryn said. "Don't you have work to do here?"

Dale rubbed the back of his neck. Damn it to hell. How did he explain the desperate worry, the ridiculous madness, the yearning inside of him?

"I'm leaving as soon as possible. All I know is that I have to see her, have to know whether she's okay. I…"

"Get ready, they're fueling the plane, I'm on my way to pick you up. I've spoken to the police, and we'll meet with them when we get there. We'll talk then."

Dale stared at the phone. Blasted Darryn. He had

planned to go to go to Mahé on his own.

For one more second, he sat frozen before he grabbed his passport and wallet. Fortunately no visas were required for the islands. And they each had a room in all their hotels with cupboards filled with clothes. This was one of those times he was very glad that he didn't have to think about packing.

Damn it, he should have stopped her from leaving. He should have been with her, he should never have let her go to Mahé on her own. He should—

Dumbfounded, he stared around his room. He was struggling to think. Doing ordinary things just didn't make sense at the moment. What was he doing in his room again?

THE INSISTENT RINGING of her phone woke Zoe up. Groggily she answered.

"How are you feeling?" Dale asked in a clipped voice.

"I… I'm fine," Zoe said and closed her eyes again. She was probably dreaming anyway.

"Darryn and I are on our way, we should be there in about seven hours. You are not to leave the hotel, okay?"

"Okay," she whispered and fell asleep again. It was so nice to hear his voice, even if it was only in her dreams.

WHEN SHE WOKE up, it was morning and Hannah was sitting on her bed.

"Hi." She smiled.

"Hi, yourself," Hannah said and scooted closer to her. "How are you feeling?"

"I'm fine. My hands are worse than my knees and they aren't so bad either. The doctor reckoned one or two of my ribs have been bruised, and that hurts like the devil, but otherwise I'm fine. My pants are ruined though." She grimaced. She held up her bandaged hands. "They look worse with the bandages, but the doctor insisted I have these on for at least a day. He'll come and check on me again this afternoon."

"I can't believe you were kicked," Hannah muttered.

"Yes, and a nasty kick too. But really, it's not so bad," Zoe said trying to erase the worry on Hannah's face. "It could have been anyone in the crowd, and it might have been done by accident."

But Hannah shook her head. "I wish it was that simple, but this was no accident."

"What is going on, Hannah? Who is this 'he' you spoke about last night and what is happening? Talk to me."

"I... I'm not sure. I have to figure this out on my own."

"But you don't have to, surely you know that we'll all help? But we can't help you if we don't know what's going on."

"And risk more of you getting hurt? I can't let that—"

A sudden commotion erupted outside their room, and the next minute both Dale and Darryn burst inside.

Zoe blinked. Hannah stood up quickly.

"What are you doing here?" Hannah demanded.

"What do you think?" Darryn said gruffly. But then Dale was next to Zoe's bed and she only had eyes for him.

"Zoe," he said and touched her face, her hair, her arms. "Are you really okay? Your hands." He breathed and turned them gently around. "What happened?"

"That's what I would also like to know," Darryn growled.

Zoe felt so overwhelmed she wanted to burst into tears. Damn it, she came to the Seychelles to get away from Dale. And now he was here, and she was so glad to see him, she wanted to throw her arms around him and sob out her worry for Hannah on his solid chest.

"You are upsetting Zoe." Hannah scolded Darryn. "Look, she's crying."

Darryn rubbed his face. "I'm sorry," he said to Zoe. "I don't want to upset you, I'm just trying to find out what happened." He turned to Hannah. "And, by the way, can I just point out that if you hadn't been so stubborn, none of this would've happened. We had security people who were happy to escort you, but, no, you always have to do things your way."

"I know that!" Hannah called out, clearly upset. "I don't need you to remind me!"

She turned to Zoe. "We'll talk later. I can't be in the same room with this man." She stormed out, Darryn close on her heels.

Shaking his head, Dale sat next to her on the bed. "Tell me what happened," he said again.

Zoe tried to remember everything and relayed the events of the previous evening in as much detail as she could.

"Hannah seems to think it was because I was mistaken for her that this happened," Zoe said. "Although she hasn't gotten around to telling me exactly why anyone would want to hurt her."

"How could someone mistake you for her?" Dale asked, obviously startled.

Zoe grimaced. "I know. She's so beautiful, blonde, and well-known, why anyone would mistake me for her, I don't know. We were wearing similar outfits, maybe that was why."

Surprised, Dale touched her cheek. "That's not what I meant at all. Yes, Hannah is beautiful, but you..." He inhaled and stroked her arms. "I don't see anyone else when you're around."

Zoe caught her breath. "Dale," she whispered.

He smiled and moved closer. "At least you're sounding better than you did when I phoned earlier."

"It was really you on the phone? I thought I was dreaming," she said and could have bitten her tongue.

He smiled. "So, you dream about me?"

"Dale, please. I'm not in the mood for teasing."

DALE PICKED UP one of her hands and played with her fingers. "When the staff here phoned me to say you'd been in an accident…"

It was so difficult to convey the absolute dread he'd felt in the pit of his stomach for hours. "They tried to explain what happened, but I didn't know how badly you were hurt and had to hear your voice. I died a thousand deaths. Zoe, I don't know what is going on between us, but this incident has just confirmed what I'd already known—I want you in my life."

Zoe was scowling. "Dale, I'm just a diversion for you—"

He swore and gently touched her face. "Is that really what you think? That I end up in bed with every woman I'm seen with? Damn it, Zoe, you left me, remember? And, okay, I have a reputation that I'm usually the one leaving, but with you… It's different."

"I… I…" She bit her lip, and all his good intentions flew out of the window.

His hands trembled. "Why? After the amazing night we had, why did you leave? You made coffee for me, left me something to eat, which by the way, has never happened to me before, but you left. Why?"

She gave him a look before she glanced down. "I left before you could," she said.

Dale stared at her back and swallowed. Time to come clean.

He nodded. "The truth? You're probably right. I would

have. I would have pushed you away because I was completely thrown by the intensity of what happened between us," he said quietly.

Her face was carefully blank. But she swallowed and he knew—he had a chance. If he didn't bugger it up again, that was.

"What do you mean?" she asked, her voice husky.

He could smile again. "You know perfectly well what I mean. The night we had together was amazing—you were amazing. It was much more than sex. I still don't know exactly what this thing is between us, but I want to find out. One night with you," he said, taking her hands in his, "has not been enough." He leaned in and kissed her softly. "And I'm not sure," he murmured against her skin, his lips gliding over her mouth, "how many nights and days would be enough."

She pulled away slightly. "I don't know, Dale, it makes working with you very complicated."

He smiled. "Then it's complicated. Come to think of it, you're complicated. You annoy me, you irritate me, you've upset my life, but I want to spend every one of those annoying, irritating, upsetting moments with you."

"I annoy you?" She gasped. "You are the most annoying person I have ever met!"

"Good." He smiled. "Then we fit perfectly."

HIS WORDS NESTLED around her heart and breathing became difficult. *We.* He'd referred to them as we. Two of them. Together.

He kissed her on the forehead and took her hands again. "Now you have to rest, please. Your bruised ribs must hurt like hell. You're still very pale. Darryn and I will talk to the police—"

"There's really nothing to tell, I—"

"We have to report the incident, and they will need to get a statement from you. But I'll come and get you later, and we'll see whether you're up to an evening out."

Dazed, Zoe stared after him. That "we" word again. She hugged herself. This could not possibly last. But for now, she was going to enjoy this beautiful island, this gorgeous man, and whatever life was handing her on a platter at the moment. Later, after Dale had moved on to the next woman, there would be enough time for crying.

Chapter Fifteen

DARRYN WAS PACING their office when Dale entered. Darryn rounded on him immediately.

"The police are on their way. What did Zoe say? What happened?"

Dale stared at his brother. He'd never seen him like this. "She repeated what our security people told us. Except she mentioned that Hannah thought whoever did this mistook Zoe for Hannah."

"What?" Darryn said, clearly upset. "I could wring that woman's neck. She didn't say anything about that to me."

"If you stop behaving like a madman, she might talk to you. Talk about crazy behavior. What the hell is wrong with you?"

Darryn swore. "Someone hurt Zoe, thinking it was Hannah. And Hannah knows something, I can see it. The hit and run incident and this one are connected in some way, I'm sure of it."

Dale frowned. "And the police? What do they say?"

"Still investigating is all the information I could get out of them. Damn it, I'm sure Hannah suspects someone, but will she talk about it? *Nooo*, the lady is too stubborn, too bloody pigheaded to tell anyone or to ask for help."

"Hmmm, she sounds like someone I know. You know, someone who is stubborn and pigheaded, not prone to ask for help—sound familiar?"

"You're the last person to talk about crazy behavior," Darryn said in a tight voice. "You got a thing for Zoe?"

"You got a thing for Hannah?" Dale asked.

"Just shut up," Darryn said and, cussing under his breath, stormed out of the office.

Dale stared at the closing door. There was obviously something going on between Darryn and Hannah, and Hannah's troubles worried him but Darryn would make sure that they found out what really happened.

But at the moment Dale's only concern was Zoe. At least he'd seen her, knew she wasn't too badly hurt. For the first time since he got the phone call, he could relax. Zoe was going to be okay, and he was going to make sure she stayed that way. She was not making a move on this island without him. Anyone who'd want to hurt her would have to go through him first.

Their secretary announced the arrival of the police. He wasn't sure what they could tell them, but he and Darryn both felt it was necessary to lodge a complaint. And to find out whether there was any information about the hit-and-run accident Hannah had been in last year.

"FEELING BETTER I see," Hannah said from the door.

Motioning Hannah to enter, Zoe finished brushing her hair. "Yes, I'm much better. Hopefully these bandages can also be removed later this afternoon." She walked towards Hannah. "Sis, who is trying to hurt you?"

Hannah sighed. "I don't know."

"But you have a good idea?"

Hannah walked towards the big windows overlooking the sea. "Maybe. I don't know. And I don't want to say anything before I do know."

"Does Darryn know what is going on?"

Hannah shook her head quickly. "No, and I don't want him to even know what I've told you."

"Is that why you didn't want to talk to the police? I couldn't tell them anything really, either. I didn't see anything. I could only describe what happened to me, but I didn't see the person who pushed and kicked me."

"Zoe, I…" Hannah's eyes filled with tears. "I only have suspicions at this point, not anything concrete for the police. I want to tell you, I really do, but …" Hannah burst into tears.

Zoe quickly walked closer and hugged Hannah. "I'm worried about you, Sis. There was the hit and run incident and now this. I really think you should talk to the police or—"

Hannah's sobs grew louder. "Zoe, please," she hiccupped. "Not now, please? I'm so glad you're going to be okay, let's not talk about this anymore?"

Zoe wanted to protest, but Hannah was clearly very upset and she didn't want to pressure her further.

She led Hannah back to the bed and gave her a tissue.

Gradually Hannah's sobs subsided. Eventually she turned to Zoe with a lopsided smile. "So, Dale arrived on his white horse when you were hurt."

"Mmm, and so did Darryn," Zoe teased.

That shut Hannah up for a couple of seconds. "It's not the same, and anyway I don't want to talk about Darryn."

Zoe thought about Darryn's extreme behavior of this afternoon. She sighed. What was it with the Cavallo men? She hadn't heard from Dale since the morning she'd left her flat after their lovemaking and yet, when she was hurt, he flew in, acting caringly. Which meant what, exactly?

"You slept with Dale?" Hannah asked.

"Yeah, I did."

"And?"

"And nothing. You know the kind of lives they lead. I'm just a diversion at the moment."

"You sure about that?" Hannah asked.

"I'm going to finish this project. By that time, he'll have someone else hanging on his arm, and I'll probably only see him at family gatherings. The only reason he asked me to do this project was as a favor to Don. We all know that. I don't like the idea that I got this assignment because of family ties, but I'm going to make sure I use the opportunity to my firm's advantage. And anyway, we know happy-ever-afters don't really exist, don't we? Men don't stick around when the going gets tough."

Hannah snorted. "You're worth being around, Zoe, I wish you knew that. Don't sell yourself short. But you're right about one thing. Men don't stick around."

"And you know that how? Darryn?"

Hannah shrugged. "It's complicated. You feeling up to a stroll outside? We'll stay on the hotel grounds," she added with a grimace.

"Yes, please. If I stay here for another minute, I'll go crazy."

Zoe stole a glance at Hannah as they took the lift down. Her sister was obviously upset and worried about something. She just hoped Hannah would know when to ask for help.

ZOE LOOKED AROUND the secretary's office. It didn't look as if anyone was there at the moment. Dale's voice came from his office in the hotel. Well, then she would have to announce her arrival herself. Nervously she walked up to the door and knocked.

She wasn't really sure why she was here, but she had to see him. The doctor had removed the bandages and she wanted to tell Dale.

Dale stopped talking and the next minute the door flew open. He had his phone in his hand.

"Zoe!" he exclaimed. "I'm just talking to Darryn, he's at the hotel on Praslin. Are you feeling okay? Shouldn't you still be in bed? What did the doctor say?"

"I'm good. The doctor said my hands are better, I've probably bruised a rib or two, but I'm fine." She smiled and held up her hands.

Dale lifted his phone. "We'll talk later," he said into the phone. He listened for a few seconds and then handed the phone to Zoe. "Darryn wants to talk to you," he said, pointing to a chair. "But do sit down, please."

Zoe sat down and put the phone to her ear. "How is Hannah? Has she told you anything else?" Darryn asked brusquely.

"No, she hasn't really. She... um... she's on her way to Mauritius," Zoe said. "The location for the shoot was moved suddenly this afternoon."

Darryn swore. "Did she ask for it to be moved?"

"Not as far as I know but—"

Darryn cussed loudly on the other end and Zoe winced. That particular sentence structure she hadn't heard before.

"How could Hannah leave the island when we're still not sure what happened?" Darryn asked.

But apparently Dale had had enough of his brother. Darryn was talking so loudly Dale could probably hear every word. He took the phone from her hand.

"You can grill Zoe later, she's still not well," he said and ended the call.

He pulled another chair closer to her. "Are you really okay?"

"I'm fine. Really," she said. "I'm worried about Hannah, though. The hit and run incident and now this, but she won't tell me anything."

"The police will keep us posted and I can promise you Darryn will not rest until this thing is resolved." He touched her arm. "If you're feeling better, may I take you out to dinner tonight?"

"That sounds great." She looked at her watch and turned to leave. "I want to call my mother, though, and want to do it now. I'm amazed she hasn't tried to call me already. I thought you'd have told Don and Caitlin what happened."

Dale shook his head. "No, we didn't want to say anything before we knew exactly what was going on. We didn't want to upset Caitlin further. She was ready to throttle Darryn and myself."

"What did you do?"

Dale laughed. "Because she blamed us for the fact that you and Hannah had left early for Mahé," he said and handed her his phone again. "Here, call your mom from my landline then I can also speak to her. She'll need reassurance and I can't give it to her."

"HANNAH HAS JUST also called me. She's not telling me everything," Zoe's mom said after Zoe told her what had happened.

Zoe grimaced. She'd tried to skim over what had really happened, but her mother was nobody's fool. To try and keep anything from their mother, was a hopeless exercise. She always knew when something was wrong. "Dale and Darryn are talking to the police, Mom. Hannah will be surrounded by people during the photo shoot on Mauritius and hopefully she'll be back home soon."

"I hope so. And how are you feeling?"

"I'm fine, Mom, really."

"And your Dale flew all the way over to Mahé because you were hurt?" her mother asked, and Zoe groaned out loud, glad Dale had stepped out to his secretary's office for the moment. Of all the things she'd just told her mother, that was what she was focusing on?

"Mom, you're such a die-hard romantic!" She laughed. "He's not my Dale. We're... I don't know what we are, but please don't start writing about fairy lights and white dresses, okay?"

Her mother inhaled sharply. "Fairy lights?" she gushed. "Of course, that's what you'll want. And you'll wear a sleek white dress in satin and lace. Oh, darling, I can just see you!"

"Mom," Zoe said, tightening her hold on the phone. "Listen to me. Nobody is getting married, please."

"Who's getting married?" Dale asked from behind her and she closed her eyes.

"Nobody. My mother is telling me about her latest romance," Zoe said. "You know she writes fairy tales for grown-ups, don't you?"

"I write romances, not fairy tales," her mother said indignantly. "Let me talk to him."

With trepidation, Zoe switched on the speaker and gave Dale the phone. She had no idea what her mother would say, but she wanted to be able to stop her when necessary.

"So, you write romances?" Dale asked her mother, his eyes twinkling. "Tell me about it?"

"Don't ask!" Zoe called out. "She'll never stop talking about it." She groaned. Of all the things to be talking about! She closed her eyes.

Her mother's voice was very clear over the phone. "Yes, I write romances. I love to write about love—there's always a new side to it I haven't discovered before. And I adore the happy endings, especially those that end with a beautiful wedding. One where fairy lights guide guests down the stairs to a small beach. Our heroine wears a satin gown, the top part covered in lace, and she has a bouquet of exquisite pink roses. The groom waits for her at the bottom of the stairs and when he sees her, he"—her mother paused dramatically—"falls in love with her all over again, because he realizes so many of his smiles begin with her. In fact, I'm writing such a scene right now."

"Oh, Mother, you've been updating your Pinterest board again, haven't you?" Zoe said, trying not to think about the scene her mother had just described. It felt all too real.

She didn't want to catch Dale's eye—he must be trying his best not to laugh out loud.

"Lovely line, I thought," her mother said.

DALE STARED AT Zoe. The line her mom had just recited echoed deep within him. It was so true—all his smiles did begin with Zoe. Corny, yes, but it explained a little of his confused feelings, things he felt but found hard to put into words. He smiled more when he was with her than he'd ever done before. And it wasn't because she was funny or wittier than other women he'd met. But somehow, when he thought of her, he ended up smiling.

"Now, Dale, what I have to say now is not meant for Zoe's ears," her mom said, and Zoe shook her head vehemently, mouthing for Dale not to switch off the speaker. He smiled and ignored her. He turned off the speaker and moved towards the windows.

"I like you, Dale Cavallo," Zoe's mom said. She lowered her voice. "My Zoe doesn't think she's worth anyone's love. The man who wants her will have to make sure she knows how deeply she is loved, how deeply she touched him."

Stunned, Dale kept the phone against his ear long after Zoe's mom had hung up.

Chapter Sixteen

ZOE CAST A furtive look in Dale's direction. They were nearly back at the hotel after a lovely dinner. He'd been quiet all evening and hadn't spoken a word since they left the restaurant. He wouldn't tell her what her mother had said to him, and she kept wondering if her mom had somehow upset him. It was never a good idea to let her mother speak to an eligible man alone, especially a man she'd decided one of her daughters wanted.

"I'm sorry about my mom. I love her dearly but whenever a man comes close to one of her daughters, she starts seeing wedding gowns and happy-ever-afters. Please just ignore her."

Dale didn't respond; he just took her hand in his and put it on his leg. Something changed in the air around them, and Zoe struggled to breathe.

"Dale?"

"I need to be with you, but you're hurt," he said gruffly and met her eyes for a second before he focused on the traffic again.

But that second was enough for her to see the want in his

eyes, to feel the heat in his hand, to experience his need for her, to understand exactly what he meant. The car increased speed and, trying to keep up, so did her heartbeat.

She couldn't speak. Desire raced through her body, heating her blood instantly, leaving her mouth dry.

Dale finally stopped, tires screeching, in front of the hotel. He got out quickly and moved around to her side while an usher raced forward to take his car keys. Someone opened her door, but she only had eyes for Dale.

He held out his hand and, feeling as if she were walking on clouds, she moved towards him.

Taking long strides, he walked towards the lift.

"Your room is closer," was all he said.

Wordlessly, they stepped into the lift. Within seconds, after the doors closed, she was in his arms and he was kissing her. Who moved first wasn't clear, but she was exactly where she wanted to be. His mouth fit so perfectly over hers, as if it had been made especially for his.

His touch was gentle, but she hungered for him and snaked her arms around his body, pulling him closer. With a groan, he hugged her gently and his hands moved eagerly up and down her back. She ignored the pain from the kick of the previous night; there was no way she was going to stop Dale from touching her.

The ping of the lift announced their arrival. Dale pulled back, blinked, and with dazed eyes, he grabbed her elbow. She giggled, his eyes flashed, and he quickly steered her towards her room. The corridor was empty, and while her trembling fingers tried to find the card to open her door, he lifted her hair and planted a kiss behind her ear.

"Found it," she whispered anxiously and handed him the key. She wouldn't be able to unlock the door. Her hands were shaking too badly.

DALE SWIPED THE card, pushed Zoe into the room, and kicked the door closed behind him. He couldn't take his eyes off her. Her pupils were dilated, her mouth wet from his kiss. He wanted his hands on her, wanted her body close to his, wanted to taste her, but, most of all, he wanted her.

He gathered her close and kissed her again, trying to rein in his wildly galloping libido. But her body curved instantly into his, her hands fisted in his hair, and he lost the struggle.

A LOW PURRING sound erupted from her throat and shot straight to his loins. A primitive need pounded through his blood; he had to get his hands on her. Greedily, his lips skimmed over her face, down her neck, and up again so he could have another taste of the small place behind her ear.

ZOE CLUNG TO him as if she was trying to absorb every little thing about this moment—the sound of their laboured breathing, the heat of his hands skimming her sides, the feel of his body against hers.

He lifted her so both her legs wrapped around his body. His lips had found hers again, and without lifting his head, he staggered forward until he gently set her on her feet next to the bed.

His eyes were dark, his face taut. "I have to touch you," he said huskily, "but I don't want to hurt you."

"I'm fine," she said and lifted her top over her head. She unhooked her short skirt and it fell silently to the ground.

Without saying anything, she turned around. On the opposite wall, a mirror reflected the two of them.

He sucked in a sharp breath at the sight of her. He skimmed his fingers against her back as he unhooked the clasp of her bra, his eyes never leaving hers in the mirror. Silently her bra fell to the ground.

He stepped closer and cupped her breasts from behind.

"Look how beautiful you are," he whispered in her ear and she looked up. It was such a sensual picture—she nearly naked, her breasts covered with his hands.

HE WALKED THEM closer to the mirror. Dale couldn't stop staring at Zoe's reflection. She was beautiful, sexy, extraordinary, and no reflection but the real blood and flesh deal. He was going to have her. If he didn't lose his mind, he was going to take her in every way possible.

He kept his one hand around a soft breast and played with a hardened nipple while his other hand moved lower and lower. Her breath caught in her throat, her legs wobbled. He pulled her closer. And all the while his hand continued its journey further down her body.

She bit her lip and he cupped her, feeling the dampness through the silk. His fingers slipped underneath the elastic so skin could touch skin. He found her nub, explored, and stroked until she was shuddering.

"Dale, please..." she moaned while her arm hooked around his head, her fingers fisting his hair.

He increased the rhythm of his hand, she bucked and he watched in awe as she lost control. That she responded to him this way, that he could bring her fulfillment, filled him with wonder. With a final shudder, she leaned against him, her arm still around his head. He'd never seen anything so beautiful before.

His blood was thundering through his body, egging him on to take her right there and then. But he wanted this to last, to make it special for her.

To calm himself, he buried his face in her hair. But the silkiness surrounded him, her scent seeped through his skin, making him lose the last hold on his sanity.

He spun her around and then pulled his shirt over his head. She smiled, and he got tangled up in the sleeves. Swearing, he plucked it over his head while her hands helped him with his belt.

"I'm aching for you," he said while kicking away his pants, "but you were hurt…"

She smiled and advanced, pushing him backwards until he fell back on the bed.

"It will work if I'm on top," she said and straddled him. He forgot to breathe.

He lifted his arms to grab her closer, but she moved back slightly. "But you have to be still," she admonished him sternly. "You can't touch me. But I…" She breathed and bent down to trail her lips over his abs. "I can do anything I want."

Dale had lost his ability to form a coherent word a while ago and could only grunt. He couldn't take his eyes off Zoe. She was obviously enjoying herself. She tasted and licked and sighed and touched every centimetre of his upper body until he was burning up.

ZOE COULDN'T BELIEVE what she was doing. She'd never done anything this bold before, she'd never wanted to before. But here, with Dale, her body simply took over and instinctively did things she'd never even thought of. She wanted to pleasure him, to drive him slowly insane the way he'd driven her crazy minutes before. All her senses were on high alert, absorbing every sensory impulse coming their way. Her blood raced through her body, heating her skin, making her weak with want.

Looking up at him through her lashes, she moved down his body, her hands exploring his hard muscles and toned flesh, her mouth enjoying his taste. Underneath her lips he was burning up, feverish, and his hands were desperately trying to grab her.

She smiled and moved away, still farther down his body until she could take him in her hand. He was throbbing for her. Breathless, she bent down to take him in her mouth, but with an oath, he lifted himself and shifted her so she was lying beneath him.

"You should know by now, if you do that, this will be over in seconds," he said hoarsely. "Let me…"

HE RAN HIS hands up, calf to thigh, felt her shuddering, and her unconscious response pushed him over the edge.

Blindly, he opened her legs so that he could enter her, become one with her. She was ready and wet for him. He slid home and buried himself deep within her. Like a silk glove, she closed around him, he whispered her name and was lost.

ZOE WOKE UP with a smile on her face. She looked over her shoulder at Dale who was trailing a finger over the sheet covering her body.

"Mmmm." She sighed and stretched. "Do I want to

know what time it is?" she asked groggily. They hadn't slept much, and this morning she ached in unfamiliar places.

"It's time," he whispered, nibbling on her shoulder, "to have you again." He slowly pushed the sheet down, and she turned around to him.

"Wait!" he called out and turned her back on her side. "What is this?" He pointed to her back.

"Oh," Zoe said and touched the place he was pointing at. "That must be where I was kicked…"

"What?" Dale said, clearly upset as he gently turned her around to have another look at the bruise. "Damn it, look at the size of this bruise. Are you okay? I'm sorry, I should have been gentler. I—"

"Dale, it's fine. I bruise easily. It will heal, it's not so bad," Zoe said and tried to turn on her back, but Dale wouldn't let her.

He moved over her, kissed her shoulder and slowly trailed his lips down her back. Without words, his lips comforted her, told her he was upset she'd been hurt.

Her throat clogged up. It was going to be so hard to say good-bye to this man. She sniffled and he stopped.

"Are you crying?"

She smiled and turned on her back, holding her arms out to him. "Happy tears," she said, pulling him down.

DALE BUTTONED UP his shirt while he stared out the window. It was the beginning of June, a beautiful day. The azure blue of the ocean around these islands never ceased to stun him. He loved the sea, always had, but here, surrounded by the clear, blue waters of the Indian Ocean, he could enjoy the vastness, the never-ending ebb and flow of it every second. The months from May to October usually brought drier, cooler weather, but the temperature rarely dipped below twenty-four degrees Celsius. And today was a typical day in paradise.

He'd just finished showering, one which took a long time because Zoe had joined him. With a groan, he closed his eyes. Hell, the woman would be the death of him yet. Would he ever be able to get enough of her? This constant hunger for a woman was not something he'd ever experienced before.

He was smiling again, he realized, and laughed out loud. It was a beautiful day, there was a gorgeous woman in the bathroom, and they were on an exotic island—he had a lot to smile about.

"You look happy," Zoe said as she walked into the room, the towel wrapped around her body.

Dale stopped breathing and stared at her. The temperature of his blood increased from zero to boiling in one second. With two long strides he reached her side and pulled her into his arms. She melted against him and he swallowed her sigh. With a soft laugh, she slipped her arms around him and he simply surrendered.

Chapter Seventeen

GROGGILY, ZOE YAWNED and opened her laptop. The last two days had been a whirlwind of sightseeing, eating, laughing, and loving. She turned to stare at Dale's sleeping form on her bed.

He was a wonderful escort, an attentive guide, a supportive friend, and a very innovative lover. She blushed just thinking about the nights they'd shared. He made her feel so special, so coveted, so beautiful that she'd let down her guard and was able to relax with him. And she liked the person she was around him.

With a sigh, she turned back to her computer. But reality was slowly intruding. She had a project to finish, a firm she had to go back to, other people were dependent on her.

And somewhere deep inside her, she had begun to wonder—how long would this fling last? Because it would end at some point. She had nothing to offer him in the long run and she was not the kind of girl men stayed with.

Dale had been quiet during dinner last night and there had been a strange urgency in his lovemaking afterwards. Was he getting bored? Had he decided it was time to move on?

Irritated with herself, she opened the plan of the hotel that Dale's office had sent her. In between their outings over the past two days, she'd begun working on her proposal and had started on sketches of what she had in mind for the bedrooms. That she had the plan made it so much easier. She'd tell Dale someone from his office had sent her them as soon as he woke up.

With everything that had happened recently, she hadn't really thought about telling him she had the plans, but now she had to. Why he didn't want her to have them in the first place, she still found so strange; surely he understood it was a vital part of getting a final proposal in place?

She glanced over at him again only to find him propped up on his elbow, staring at her, the strangest look on his face.

"Dale?" She slowly got up.

"Come here," he ordered her.

She lifted an eyebrow but obeyed. When she reached his side, he grabbed her hand and pulled her down on him.

"I want you," he said, raining kisses all over her face. "I sleep and I dream of wanting you, I wake up and I have to have you..." he murmured against her mouth, his eyes hot, his touch impatient.

His lips captured hers and he pulled at her gown until it fell open.

His tongue slipped into her mouth, his hands gathered her close and she forgot to think, to rationalize, to worry.

She could only feel.

FROWNING, DALE WALKED around the bed, looking for his shoes. What exactly was going on here? He felt excited, he couldn't wait for Zoe to finish in the bathroom so he could see her again, touch her again, be with her again. This after a whole night of being with her. Make that two nights and two days of being with her. Damn it, he wasn't a bloody schoolboy!

He'd been so distraught when he heard she'd been hurt, there wasn't time to think. He had let his emotions dictate all his actions—never a good business policy. But now he found himself unable to think of anything else besides Zoe, unable to make any plans that didn't include her, unable to think of a future without her in it. And, bloody hell, it was freaking him out. Yes, he wanted her in his life, but damn it, she didn't have to take it over.

He'd not been looking for this kind of complication in his life. There was a new hotel to furnish, another one to plan. He didn't have time to walk around, smiling like an idiot all the time because he couldn't stop thinking about a woman.

He bent down, picked up his shoes, and walked to a chair that stood in front of a small table. While he fastened the laces, he saw Zoe's laptop was open. She'd been working on it earlier; he absently clicked to activate the screen.

His hand froze, his breath left his body when he saw what was lit up on the small screen. It was a plan of the new hotel. The one he'd told her she couldn't have. He checked the email heading. It was sent from one of the intern's computers it seemed.

Rage raced through him. Damn it to hell! He should've known he couldn't trust her. She'd asked for the plan behind his back. After he'd specifically told her she could work in his offices on it.

"How come you're dressed?" he heard her voice from the doorway of the bathroom.

He didn't turn to look at her.

"I see you got the plan," he said as calmly as he could.

"Yes, I was just about to tell you. I phoned your office to ask your secretary. She was out, but the person who answered the phone sent it to me. Dale, I can't work without it, you know that."

Finally, he turned around to look at her. She was tying the knot on her short, sexy robe. She was without makeup and she looked so young, and all he wanted to do was to get her naked again as quickly as possible. He turned away from her.

"I told you very clearly that if you needed the plans, you'd have to come to our offices."

"Dale, please listen? I've never had to work without a plan of an office building or a hotel before. I need the measurements, the... Damn it, I don't have to tell you. You know."

"You went behind my back to an intern—"

"Like you went behind my back to get Susan to sign the contract?"

"It's not the same thing!"

"Oh, really?"

"What I do know is that I can't trust you—"

She gasped. "How can you say that after the last two days?" Her eyes were wet with tears.

"So because I showed you the islands, had sex with you, you thought you can do things behind my back? I really thought you were different. But you've just been using me. You never wanted to do this job in the first place but saw it as an opportunity to further your career. Hell, you even went so far as to sleep with me. But guess what? This is over. You're fired. Forget the contract, you're free to leave. I can't work with someone who does things behind my back, and I definitely can't be with someone who's only interested in what I can do for her." He snarled and opened the door.

"You've found a reason," she said softly.

Furious, he glanced back at her. "What the hell are you talking about?"

"You've had enough of me, you were looking for a reason to end this and now you've found one."

"That is not what this is about!" he shouted.

She shrugged. "It's fine, Dale. You've never wanted me to work on this project to begin with. Why you insisted

Susan sign a contract is something I'll probably never understand. Whatever else there has been between us is obviously over. As you've told me before, I'm not even your type. I'll leave as soon as I get a flight."

Dale stared at her for another heartbeat. Somewhere inside him a little voice shouted that he was making a mistake, but she'd gone behind his back, damn it. Before he could change his mind, he stormed out of her room. He needed distance to think.

ZOE STOOD SILENTLY and waited for the door to slam behind Dale's back. The sound reverberated through her room. A sharp pain edged in just below her heart. She was right, she knew it. The plan on her computer was just an excuse. He'd been looking for a reason to leave; he got one. She should have known. Why would he stick around?

She wiped the tears from her cheeks. Why was she crying, for goodness' sake? He wasn't worth it. No man was worth it. The first thing to do was to book a plane ticket home. Slowly she sat down on the bed.

Her phone rang. It was Caitlin. Don must have finally told her what had happened.

"I'm fine," she said before Caitlin could utter a word.

"I'm glad to hear that. I'm so angry with all of you! Don has only told me a few minutes ago you'd been hurt. I can't believe you all kept this from me, even Mom. Are you really okay?"

Zoe smiled and wiped her tears away. She didn't want to upset Caitlin.

"You're pregnant, Sis. You have enough to worry about. I'm really fine. I'm a little bruised up but have nearly healed completely."

"Is there an ongoing police investigation?" Caitlin asked.

"We spoke to them, but they don't have much to go on really. Hannah has left for Mauritius, and I didn't really know what to tell them. I didn't see anything. I think the hotel's security people are also looking into it." She wasn't sure how much Don had told Caitlin and didn't want to add Hannah's notion that Hannah was the person who should've been hurt.

"If you're feeling fine, why are you crying?" Caitlin asked. "What else happened? Did Dale do something?"

Zoe sniffled. She never could keep anything from her older sister. She promptly burst into tears. "He… really hurt me, Caitlin, but I'm okay." She hiccupped. "I'm coming back and have to book a plane ticket, but I can't concentrate and I—"

"I'm in front of my computer, I'll book the flight for you. You pack, someone will take you to the airport, I'll be waiting on this side."

Chapter Eighteen

DALE PACED IN front of the windows of the big office he and his brothers shared in the hotel on Mahé. He'd spent the day at their hotel on Praslin; he couldn't stay in the same one where Zoe was. Now it was early evening and he felt restless.

He had made the right decision, damn it. Zoe knew he didn't want her to have a copy of the plans, but she went ahead and got it anyway. He couldn't work with someone like that, and he certainly couldn't be in a relationship with someone he didn't trust.

So why wasn't he elated about the whole thing, glad it was over, looking up any of the willing women in the hotel?

The door to his office flew open and Darryn strolled in. "Don is looking for you, why don't you answer your damn phone?"

Dale took out his phone and saw there were about five missed calls from Don. Damn it, he'd put his phone on silent. He didn't want to talk to anybody today, least of all to Don.

"I heard Zoe has left? What happened?" Darryn asked.

"Last time I saw the two of you, you couldn't keep your hands to yourself. I'm telling you, those Sutherland women are trouble."

Darryn's phone rang. He handed it to Dale. "It's Don again. He's looking for you."

Dale swore but took the phone.

Don was livid. "I told you, if you mess with Zoe, you mess with me," Don's voice boomed over the line.

Dale straightened, heartily fed up with the whole thing. "I didn't mess with her. I told her if she needed the plans, she'd have to come to the office. She went behind my back and got them anyway. She just used me! I can't work with someone like that, damn it!"

"Just so I'm clear, we're talking about the plans for the hotel near the Kruger?"

"Yes, of course we are."

"And you don't want to give the plans to the person who has to know every little detail of the place in order to come up with a proposal for the interior? And when she asked someone else for it, who by the way, seems to have a much better understanding of how this works, you fire her? Are you insane? Who does that?"

Behind him Darryn started laughing.

Swearing, Dale gave him the finger.

"She got to you, you poor bastard, and you don't even

know it." Darryn got up, pushed his chair back, and grabbed the phone from Dale's hand to talk to Don.

"Dale has that same stunned expression on his face you had before you realized you'd been snared. You're a sorry lot, all of you." He laughed as he handed the phone back to Dale.

"Look, I don't know what the hell is going on over there, all I care about is that my wife is upset. And I don't want that. You better fix this, Dale, and quickly." Don growled in his ear and ended the call.

"I don't know why everyone finds this so strange," Dale said, highly irritated with his brothers. "After that incident with Tammy, I never let my plans out of my sight, you all know that."

Darryn was still smiling and shaking his head. "Let me get this straight. You fired Zoe, a well-known interior decorator with a pristine reputation—your words—and the person you have chosen to work with, because she wanted the plans to the hotel she has to decorate because she wants to… what? Sell them? Give them to someone else?"

"Damn it, it's not that. It's just she… I…" He tried, but now that he had to put his fears into words, it sounded so farfetched and so, well, ridiculous.

Darryn slapped him on the shoulder. "Exactly. You're behaving like a damn fool because you fell for this woman. And because it scared the hell out of you, you used the first excuse to get her out of your life. Right?"

Dale stared at him. "I didn't fall for anybody. She used me to further her own career, damn it. I can't work with someone I can't trust, let alone have a relationship with her."

"Oh, so now we're talking about a relationship?" Darryn grinned. "And sorry to burst your inflated ego, but from what I hear, Zoe doesn't need your job to further her career. Her firm has been doing very well without you. I'm taking the plane and flying back tonight. Are you coming with me?"

Dazed, Dale shook his head. He had to see Zoe again. Hopefully, she was still on the island even if she'd left the hotel. Darryn left, muttering under his breath.

Dale sat down on the nearest chair. Zoe was right—he had been looking for a way out, and, yes, what he felt when he was around her scared the hell out of him, just as Darryn had said.

He didn't do relationships. He liked Zoe, found her attractive, he'd spent time with her, enjoyed her in bed, but it had to have ended at some point, right? He was not in the market for marriage, babies and white picket fences.

Suddenly the picture in his head was real and he was chasing a giggling, chubby-legged little girl on a lawn, a cocker spaniel yapping at their heels. Stunned, he dropped his forehead in his hands. The little girl had Zoe's laugh, her hair, her eyes.

Something inside him moved. Of course. He liked her, yes, but much more than that, he loved her. He loved everything about her. A smile threatened to split his face in two. Why had it taken him so long to make sense of his feelings?

He jumped up, not sure what to do next. Of course he loved her. It was that simple and that complicated. Simple, because she'd touched his soul the minute he'd laid eyes on her all those months ago, and he'd fallen in love with her at that precise moment. Complicated, because he'd messed up the whole thing and had some serious groveling to do. He winced. He'd even accused her of using him!

TWENTY MINUTES LATER, Dale was cursing a blue streak while he was trying to get Darryn on the line. Finally, his brother picked up.

"She's left!" Dale called out, giving voice to his frustration. "I went looking for her but she's already left on a flight, damn it. What time are you leaving?"

"I assume we're talking about Zoe?" Darryn asked, clearly amused.

"Yes, I'm talking about Zoe. She's gone. I can't believe she just left without telling me!"

Darryn barked out a laugh. "You fired her, isn't that right?"

"Yes, but I didn't know then what I know now!"

"You have it bad, don't you, you poor sod? Hurry up, we're just about to take off."

Dale grabbed his wallet and sprinted for the door. He

had to get to Zoe as soon as possible. The same urgency that had brought him to Mahé in the first place was back. The only difference was—this time he was the one responsible for hurting her.

ZOE LIFTED HER bag from the carousel and fell behind the other passengers walking down the long corridor. The only thing preventing her from bursting into tears was the knowledge Caitlin would be waiting on the other side of the sliding doors.

The past twelve hours were a blur. Someone had come to her room to pack her things; dazed, she'd followed the friendly woman down to reception where someone else was waiting to take her to the airport. Just before she left the hotel, she remembered she hadn't paid, but when she'd offered her card card, she was told it had been taken care of. There was a lot she had to thank Caitlin for.

She'd walked down corridors, waited in long queues, handed over her ticket, found a seat. For seven hours she stared out of the window. She couldn't sleep, she couldn't eat, couldn't drink. The pain, lodged just below her heart, was worse than her aching ribs and filled her whole being, making it impossible to think of anything else.

The sliding doors opened and she looked around frantically for Caitlin. She couldn't see her sister. Maybe she should try and phone her...

"Zoe," she heard a voice behind her and turned quickly. For a minute, she'd thought it was Dale, but it was his brother Don, Caitlin's husband.

"This way," he said and took her arm.

She felt like crying. The last person she wanted to see was Don. He and Dale looked so much alike and she didn't want to be reminded of the person who'd ripped her heart out.

"Caitlin..." she got out before she had to swallow the lump in her throat.

"Waiting in the car for you. The airport was so busy when we arrived, and I didn't want her to stand around for too long." He smiled sheepishly. "I'm a bit overprotective, she tells me."

Zoe tried to smile, but her throat clogged up again. She concentrated on following Don. He was besotted with his wife and didn't even try to hide it. It would seem as if Caitlin's fairy tale might just be one long happy-ever-after. At least one of them would get to live out their mother's stories.

"Look, I don't want to make excuses for my brother, there is no real justification for his behavior. But I would like to tell you about the intern we had a few years ago who screwed him over. It's no excuse but explains his paranoia when it comes to his plans."

Zoe listened as Don told her what the intern had done. Yes, it made sense that he would be distrustful of strangers wanting to see his plans. But she'd given her body to him, she wasn't a stranger. He should at least have known enough about her to know he could trust her.

She lifted her head and tried to breathe. People were milling around, and the airport was busy as always. Six days ago, she'd also been here, trying to get away from Dale. But then he'd come to her rescue, and she'd spent the most amazing few days and nights with him.

Maybe a few days of bliss were all most people got. She'd never forget the magic of those few days.

But she never wanted to be hurt like this again. Ever. A body could only handle so much pain in one lifetime. She had her work, her mom, her sisters and, now and then, her dad. That would be her life. And in the bigger picture, it wasn't such a bad one after all.

Chapter Nineteen

B Y THE TIME Dale started hammering on Don's front door, he was frantic. He and Darryn had arrived too late last night to call anyone. But since early this morning he had been trying to get hold of Zoe.

She wasn't answering her phone. She hadn't been at her flat or at work. Susan, the woman who worked with her, didn't even know Zoe was back.

He'd tried Hannah's phone, but there was no answer, and the hotel in Mauritius had said she was busy with a shoot.

Because he didn't have Zoe's mother's cell number, he'd phoned every Sutherland in the book in Hermanus but couldn't get hold of her. She either didn't have a landline or it wasn't listed. He'd tried to phone Caitlin, but she kept slamming the phone down.

So here he was. Don would probably kill him, but Dale was beyond caring. He had to get hold of Zoe, he had to tell her how he felt.

He was still hammering when the door flew open. A very grim Caitlin frowned at him.

"What do you want, Dale? You should be very glad Don isn't here right now, he's ready to wring your neck. That is, of course, after I finish with you." She hadn't raised her voice, but ice dripped from every word.

Dale rubbed his face. He hadn't slept in hours and was feeling faint, but he had to make Caitlin understand.

"You don't understand—"

"You're right. I don't understand why you would accuse Zoe of using you, of stealing your plans. She doesn't need you or your bloody plans. You're my brother-in-law and I love you, but right now I don't like you very much, so it's best if you just go." She started to close the door.

"But I'm in love with her!" Dale shouted and the door stopped.

Caitlin's face still didn't show any emotion, but the door wasn't closing on him any longer. He had a chance. Going for broke seemed to be the only way out of this mess.

"I know I've screwed up. I know I've hurt her. But you see, I was so dense, I didn't know this craziness inside of me was because I'd fallen in love with her way back the first time I saw her—in my mom's restaurant. You remember that day? She was wearing a turquoise top with this ridiculously short white skirt, and I just..." His words dried up. Mere words couldn't convey the depth of his feeling.

A soft hand touched his, and he looked up into Caitlin's face. She was smiling and was pulling him inside.

"You men are so dense," she said exasperated. In the

kitchen, she pushed him onto one of the barstools.

"When last did you eat?" she asked while switching the kettle on.

Dazed, Dale stared at her. Eat? He hadn't thought about food since yesterday morning.

"Thought so. Let's get some food into you," Caitlin said and started pulling plates from the cupboard as she kept up a running conversation.

"What you Cavallos don't understand is that, as far as ordinary people are concerned, you come from a different planet where money is never an issue, where people are always nice to you because you have money and, in most instances, they're only nice because they want something from you. For that reason, you treat everyone with suspicion and, I don't know, it's like you're waiting for people to do something so that you can prove you're right. My sisters and I come from a very different background. We don't use people."

"I know that…"

"And," she said, turning around to look him straight in the eye, "from what I can gather, you've slept with Zoe, you've spent time with her, which means you have to know at least the basic things about her. Like the fact that she doesn't use people. It's rather the other way around, she happily lets people use her. She doesn't realize her own worth—it probably has to do with our dad walking away when we were still little, I don't know. I had trust issues because of that, and Zoe has somehow decided it was because she wasn't the kind of girl anyone would want to stay around for. An idiot boyfriend when she was a student confirmed her idea that she isn't worthy of anyone's love. She found him in bed with someone else. So you telling her all those horrible things only reinforced that belief."

Dale stared at Caitlin, only now fully aware of how deeply he'd hurt Zoe.

"What do I do?" he finally said. "I'm prepared to grovel and do whatever else I need to do. But I have to get her back."

"Why?" Caitlin asked.

"I told you!" he called out. "Because I love her!"

"And?" she asked.

"What do you mean?"

Caitlin shook her head and pushed a plate of sandwiches in front of him. "You love her… and? What? You want to be with her? Want to what?"

Dale rubbed his face. What the hell? He'd said he loved her, what the hell was Caitlin going on about?

"What are you doing here?" Don's voice thundered from the doorway. "Are you upsetting my wife?" he bellowed, and with long strides, he walked up to Caitlin and folded his arms around her before he fixed his blazing eyes on Dale.

Caitlin laughed and patted his cheek. "It's fine, my darling, relax. He loves Zoe." She smiled and kissed her husband.

"What?" Don asked while his wife was kissing him.

"He loves Zoe, that's why he's behaving like a lunatic." She smiled wider. "Remember what you were like?"

Don hugged his wife to him. "That certainly explains a lot," he said, but he was not smiling. "But that's still no excuse for the way you've treated her."

"I know, okay, I know!" Dale got up. "But I have to get her back. I don't know how to go on without her. She'd somehow reached into my soul and rearranged my wiring. I need her to be able to function properly. But I can't even get hold of her. I don't know where she is!" He was sounding desperate, but at this point he didn't care.

"She's with our mom in Hermanus," Caitlin said.

"Well, then I'll go to her," he said and turned to leave.

Caitlin grabbed his arm. "Think about what I asked you. You said you love her. But what then?"

"I have to get to her, I don't know what you're talking about," he muttered and stormed out of the house.

Behind him he could hear Don roaring with laughter. There was nothing to laugh about, so what the hell was wrong with everybody?

IT WAS COLD. Zoe pulled her parka closer around her body. She was walking on Grotto Beach, one of the beautiful beaches of Hermanus. The sky was overcast, the sea stormy, the waves angry. It was June, the middle of winter and, typical of this time of the year, it had been raining since she'd arrived yesterday. When there was a break in the weather, she jumped at the chance to get out of her mother's house.

Caitlin and Don had ignored her request to be taken to her flat in Green Point yesterday and had brought her straight through to her mother in Hermanus. Her usually happy and chattering mother was quiet, ran a bath for her, bundled her into bed, and had plied her with tea and soup. Zoe had finally fallen asleep.

The wounds on her hands had healed almost completely. What she could do about the wound inside of her, though, she had no idea. There wasn't a bandage big enough to cover the hole, and she couldn't think of an ointment that would ease the pain.

In spite of all the horrible things he'd accused her of, she missed Dale. She missed everything about him—the way his hand would automatically find hers when they were walking, the way his eyes crinkled when he laughed, the way he smiled when he saw her, the way he touched her body, the way he kissed her.

A sob escaped and she pressed her hand against her lips. Her heart had been broken into a million tiny pieces—how did one fix that?

Part of her daily job as an interior decorator was to make sure things worked out, to double-check that everything was going according to plan, that orders that had been placed were delivered—she fixed glitches, she solved problems. But she didn't know how to fix her heart.

Her feet stopped walking. The roaring of the waves slowly receded as the one thought she'd just had exploded in her brain. Her heart was broken. A heart could only break when a person loved someone.

Zoe sobbed out a laugh and hugged herself. Of course she loved the idiot, she'd always loved him.

It started to rain again. She lifted her face up and closed her eyes, letting the rain wash her tears away while the pain inside her body increased with every cold raindrop.

She'd always known he'd walk away. It was going to happen sooner or later. And maybe it was better that it was sooner. And maybe, someday, after the hole in her insides had closed up, she was going to meet a wonderful man. One who loved her for who she was, one who understood her soul, one... how did her mother put it again? One whose smiles began with her.

She grimaced. *And pigs will fly.* Yeah, right. Fed up with herself, she stomped back to her car. If Dale didn't want her, fine. She should have told him about asking for the plans, but if he'd told her about the bloody intern, she'd have understood and maybe they could have worked something out. But the fact was, he hadn't spoken to her about anything of importance, really.

And he obviously hadn't bothered to get to know her at all, otherwise he would not have accused her of all the things he had. Which meant he was the idiot.

Chapter Twenty

DALE LIFTED HIS hand to knock on the front door of Zoe's mother's house in Hermanus. From here he had a beautiful view of Walker Bay. The greyness of the clouds was picked up by the water, turning the sea into a dark mass that seemed to go on forever. It echoed what was going on inside of him.

Without Zoe there was no colour in his life. Why had it taken him so long to realize that?

The door opened before his knuckles could connect with the panel.

"Hello, Dale," Zoe's mother said, the smile he was used to seeing on her face gone for the moment.

He opened his mouth to start his apology, but she pinned him down with a look that made him forget his words. For minutes she stared into his face. And then, miraculously, her smile appeared and she held out a hand to him.

"Now I see. You love her?" she asked simply.

Relieved, Dale nodded. "Yes, I do."

"Come in," she said and opened the door wider. "You

remember the way?"

Dale nodded and walked down the short corridor to the big lounge overlooking the ocean.

"You look as if you could do with some tea. Or do you prefer something stronger?"

Dale turned back to her, shaking his head. "I don't want anything, I just want... Zoe."

She smiled. "Of course you do. She'll be back soon, she went for a walk. Please sit."

Dale sat down but couldn't relax. He had to explain. "I've hurt Zoe. I've said terrible things to her and—"

"Are you here to apologize or are you here to tell her how you feel about her?"

"Both," Dale said.

"I've told you before that the man who wants Zoe will have to make her understand how deeply he loves her. She will have to believe the guy is in it for the long haul."

"I love her, I do." Dale said, frowning. "But other than telling her that, I'm not sure what I can do. It's up to her whether she believes me."

"If it was any other woman, I would've agreed with you. But we're talking about Zoe. Their dad left when they were little. It affected all three of my girls in various ways. Caitlin had trust issues, which she had to sort out before she could trust Don, and Zoe doesn't believe she's worthy of anyone's love."

"So, what do I do?" he asked. "Please tell me, because I

need her in my life. Permanently."

Her smile lit up the whole room and her eyes glittered. "This is why I write love stories." She sniffled. "You know what to do, I'm so glad and, of course, you have my blessing."

Dale frowned, not quite sure why he needed her blessing.

"I hear her footsteps," Zoe's mother said and got up.

With his heart nearly jumping out of his chest, Dale slowly got to his feet. He made huge deals every day of his life, he took risks, he negotiated and bargained with hardcore businessmen, but he had always been sure of himself, sure about what he was putting on the table. But today, his love for Zoe was the item on the agenda, his heart the currency, and he wasn't sure about his bargaining powers at all.

Zoe was nearly at the gate before she noticed the car. Dale's car. Her heart skidded to a halt before it began beating to an erratic rhythm. She combed her fingers through her hair. She was a mess. Her eyes were probably red-rimmed, she was wearing an old pair of jeans and an ancient jersey underneath her parka.

What the hell. He'd probably thought up some more nasty things to say to her, so what she looked like was not important.

She hung the parka on the hook near the front door and slowly walked towards the lounge.

Both her mother and Dale were standing, her mother was smiling broadly. Dale looked as if someone had punched him in the gut. Hard.

Good.

"Zoe, guess who came looking for you," her mother said and waved her in. "I'm making tea. Dale wants to talk to you." She walked towards the kitchen. Just before she walked through the door, she made big eyes at Zoe behind Dale's back.

Zoe ignored her. Not even her romance-loving mother could do anything to make Zoe feel better at the moment.

"What do you want, Dale?" she asked and focused on the top button of his shirt rather than his eyes.

"Zoe, I—" he began and came closer.

She held out a hand. "Stay where you are. You can say what you came to say from over there."

Dale stopped. "I'm sorry about the things I've accused you of. You were right—I was freaked out by what was happening between us and I used the first excuse to push you away. But—"

"Dale, save it. Apology accepted. We had a fling or whatever you want to call it. It's over. And I'm actually glad I'm not under contract with you anymore, it will give me more time for the other projects we're working on. We don't have to see one another too often. Maybe the odd Christmas, but I'm sure we could handle that. Now, if you'll excuse me, I'm cold, I want to take a shower. Good day," she said and turned to leave.

DUMBFOUNDED, DALE STARED at Zoe's retreating back.

What the hell? With two long strides, he reached her and turned her around to face him. "I am not leaving before I've said what I've come here to say."

Zoe looked at him through narrowed eyes. "You've apologized, what more do you want to say?"

"I love you," he blurted out. "That's what I've come here to say. I. Love. You." He said each of the words slowly, waiting for her to swallow, to blink, to show some sort of response.

Zoe cocked her head. "Oh, you love me? So now what? You want a few more romps in bed?" She sighed. "Look, Dale, sooner or later you're going to find another excuse not to be with me. It happens. Men don't stick around. I know that. So, thank you, but no thanks." She turned around and stormed out of the room.

Bewildered, Dale stared after her. What the bloody hell?

Zoe's mother opened the kitchen door. "Did you tell her?"

"Yes, I told her, but she's stormed away," he said and put his hands on his hips.

An emptiness filled his heart. She obviously didn't feel the same way. Somehow he'd never factored that possibility into the whole thing.

"What exactly did you say to her?" Zoe's mother asked and slowly came closer.

"That I love her. I said the words. But she clearly doesn't

feel the same way," he muttered and looked around for his car keys. "I'm sorry that I've bothered you."

Zoe's mother sighed dramatically. "Oh, you men!" she called out, exasperated. "Let me walk you out."

Dale turned and walked out of the room, out of the house, out of Zoe's life. This was it.

"I thought you knew what you had to tell her," Zoe's mother said, and he stopped halfway down the stairs.

"What more could I say?" he asked, fed up, hurt and upset.

"Did you tell her you want her in your life? Permanently?"

"I've told her I love her," he called out, his frustration boiling over. "Surely that implies the rest!"

Zoe's mother smiled and patted his shoulder. "You'll figure out what to do, but"—she sighed and smiled—"because you're a man, it's probably going to take you a while, and in the meantime, my Zoe is hurting. I'm going to put my nose where it doesn't belong and will spell out for you what needs to be done. And I'll talk to your mother."

"My mother?" Dale asked, flabbergasted. "What does she have to do with anything?"

"Everything, of course! This is what you have to do, and I know just the place where it all should happen," Zoe's mother said enthusiastically and began explaining.

EVEN THOUGH SHE was trying not to cry, the tears simply streamed down her cheeks, mixing with the water from the shower. Giving up, Zoe leaned against the wall and sobbed on her arm. Loved her? He didn't know what that meant, the idiot!

Coming here and telling her he loved her when... She lifted her head and stared at the tiles for long minutes while the water still sprayed down on her. He told her he loved her. In so many words. He'd flown all the way from Mahé, had driven all the way from Cape Town to come and tell her that. She'd been so hurt about the way he'd stormed out of her life, so angry at him that she hadn't really comprehended what he told her minutes ago.

Slowly, she closed the tap, folded a towel around her and sat on the edge of the bath. Her brain cells were scrambling to make sense of what had happened.

Dale loved her. At least that was what he'd said. Could she believe him? And how long would it last? Was it really possible to love someone for the rest of their life? And when he walked away eventually? What then?

"Zoe, are you okay?" her mother asked from the other side of the door.

"Come in, Mom, I'm fine," Zoe said and her mother entered.

"Dale has left," her mother said. "What did he want to tell you?"

Zoe swallowed and tried to blink back the tears that were

threatening to spill over again. "As if you don't know." Zoe sniffled. "He says he loves me."

Her mother smiled and touched Zoe's hair. "Of course he does, my sweet girl. What's not to love about you? So why did you send him away?"

Exasperated, Zoe tried to comb out her wet hair with her fingers. "At some point, he'll leave, Mom. Isn't that what men do? I know the heroes in your stories promise they'll be around forever. But does it ever happen in real life? I mean, Dad left. And surely at some point he thought he loved you. What happened? Why do they leave?"

Her mother sighed and sat on the toilet seat. "Zoe, my dear girl, life doesn't come with any guarantees. And you can't let what your dad did affect the rest of your life, all your decisions. He and I got married when we were very young. We grew apart. Unfortunately, it happens. But there are also many other examples where couples stay together." She smiled. "Sometimes, like in my stories, men stay for the long haul."

"Not even Dad wanted to stay around me. Why would any other man want to?"

Her mother took her hand. "Your dad left me, not you girls, surely you know that? He has his flaws, we all do. But he loves you very much, you must know that?"

Zoe sniffled and tried a smile. "I know. And I know I probably have, okay make that definitely have, daddy issues. But I don't want to sit around wondering when the guy will leave, so I do the leaving before he does. But this time…" The tears spilled over. "I didn't even see it coming. I thought we had another few days…"

"Dale is just your typical male, my dear. He probably had a huge fright when he realized how he felt about you. But give the poor guy a break. He flew back from Mahé and drove from Cape Town to come and tell you how he feels." She combed Zoe's wet hair back with her fingers. "How do you feel about him?"

The tears fell down in earnest. "I love him," she said trying to wipe them away. "I've only discovered that half an hour ago."

"Then what is the problem?" her mother called out and jumped up.

"We come from such different worlds, Mom. He'll get bored with me, or something. It can't last," Zoe whispered. "What if I get hurt?"

"What if you don't?" Her mother smiled. "Come on, enough of this crying. Tell you what. You and I are going out for a pizza, my treat, and tomorrow I'm driving you back to Cape Town. I have to be back here on Friday, but we can do something fun tomorrow night, what do you say? I'll check, but I think Hannah is still in Mauritius, but we can get Caitlin and maybe ask Dana to join us. Now that Caitlin is married and not around so often, I so seldom see Dana and I miss her. During their high school years, she stayed with us most of the time, she's like another daughter to me."

Dazed, Zoe nodded. Her mother in planning mode was quite scary. But at this point it was much easier to just agree with everything. She didn't have the energy for anything else. And meeting up with Caitlin and Dana would be nice.

"And you, my dear girl, can take time to listen to your heart. The heart always knows what is right." She smiled.

Zoe rolled her eyes and followed her mother out of the bathroom. "Another pin on your Pinterest board, Mom?"

But later that night she thought about her mother's words again while staring at the ceiling.

The message from her heart was very clear. Her heart wanted Dale. It had taken her a while to realize that, but the man had touched something in her the first time she'd seen him. Her soul had recognized him as *the one* long before she was able to connect all the dots.

She loved him. She wanted him in her life. The question now was, how did she go about getting him back? How-to-get-rid-of-a-guy—now that strategy she had down pat. It was with the getting-him-to-stay part she'd always had difficulty with.

Chapter Twenty-One

B Y THE TIME Dale got home, his head was reeling. But he still had the stupid grin on his face as he dropped his bag and sat on his bed. The smile that had started while Zoe's mom was telling him what to do.

He fell backwards. Why women had to make things so complicated he had no idea. He loved Zoe. He'd told her. But apparently that hadn't been enough. Surely if he told a woman he loved her, she would know what he wanted?

His phone rang. Without lifting his head, he answered. It was Don.

"Hear your trip to Hermanus didn't go so well," Don said, not quite succeeding in hiding his laughter. He'd obviously heard about the whole thing from his mother-in-law.

"Did you know?" Dale asked. "With Caitlin. Did you know to ask?"

Don laughed. "It took me a heartbeat to know what I wanted. If it's the right woman, you don't want anything less. Hang on, Caitlin wants to talk to you too."

"I tried to tell you," Caitlin scolded, but he could hear

the smile in her voice.

"Well, hell. I knew what I was going to do. But I didn't know I had to spell out every single bloody thing."

"We women are strange that way. We need to know things. Exactly." Caitlin giggled. "But you'll learn. And Dale?"

"Yeah?"

"I didn't mean it when I said I don't like you. I do."

Still smiling, Dale put down the phone after Don had insisted on speaking to him again. He wanted to give him some more pointers, as he'd called it.

Tomorrow was going to be a crazy day. There was still some groveling to be done among all the other things. But for now, he was happy to lie here knowing he had a chance to get the girl. The one who'd touched his soul.

HER MOTHER AND Dana chatted nonstop all the way from Hermanus. Zoe had opted to sit in the back of the car. The frantic workings in her brain had finally calmed down. She had to talk to Dale. He did say he loved her. She was hanging on to the thought for dear life. The how and the when weren't quite clear at this point, but she'd figure it out.

"Isn't it a beautiful day?" Her mother sighed as they rounded the last corner over Sir Lowrys Pass. Stretched out before them was the breathtaking view of False Bay. Today, the sea was a deep, clear blue.

"Beautiful." She and Dana sighed.

"So, Dana, have you heard from David Cavallo again?" Zoe's mother asked.

Dana gasped. "Why would you think that?" she asked, clearly flabbergasted.

"Mother, really!" Zoe called out from behind. "Sorry, Dana, it's because you're like a sister to us. So, to Mom you're another daughter, that's why she feels entitled to interfere in your life."

Her mother gigged. "Dana is part of the family, she doesn't mind. I saw the way he danced with you at Caitlin and Don's wedding." She wiggled her eyebrows.

"He used to be a journalist. You know how I feel about those. And anyway, I… we…" Dana stuttered.

Zoe groaned out loud. "Mother, seriously. Dana, just ignore her. I thought she'd stopped playing matchmaker after Caitlin got married. But no such luck. She's busy with me as well."

Dana laughed and looked at Zoe's mother. "Tell me?"

"Please don't get her going," Zoe pleaded from behind them, but her mother just ignored her.

"Dale told her he loved her. And she loves him."

Dana whipped around to face Zoe. "What? Does Caitlin know? When are you getting married? Why hasn't anyone told me yet? When did this happen, for crying out loud!"

"Zoe is still dissecting the whole thing to death," Zoe's mother teased.

Dana touched her hand. "You scared?"

"Petrified," Zoe whispered.

"So? What now?" Dana asked.

"Still thinking about it," Zoe said.

"Well, while you're busy overthinking a simple thing, I booked us a table for tonight," her mother said. "But it's a surprise, I'm not telling you where. We're going shopping this afternoon, my treat."

"NERVOUS?" HIS MOTHER asked and Dale shook his head.

"No, I'm not." He smiled.

"Good, because I think they've arrived."

Dale froze. This was it. He was going to see Zoe in a few minutes and…

"Go on, go get your woman," Don teased and pushed him forward.

DANA HAD BEEN telling her about a book she'd read and Zoe hadn't taken notice of where they were going for dinner. It was only when her mother stopped the car that she looked through the window.

She stared at the name of the restaurant.

Rosa's. Dale's mother's restaurant.

"Mom," she barely got out.

Her throat was dry, her legs felt like lead. This was too

soon. She hadn't worked out quite what she wanted to say to Dale, how she was going to say it.

There was no way she could face him now; she wasn't ready.

"Come on, sweetheart." Her mom smiled and got out of the car.

And then Dale came strolling out of the restaurant. He looked magnificent. In jeans and a dark blue shirt, he was drop-dead gorgeous and sexy as sin. Her poor heart skidded to a dead stop, did a backflip before it valiantly tried to work again so that she could breathe.

He smiled at her mom and at Dana, opened Zoe's door, and held out his hand.

"Zoe," he said, looking as if nothing could faze him.

Dumbstruck, and without taking her eyes from his, Zoe took his hand. And she felt the slight tremor under his skin. Her shoulders relaxed. He was as unsure of what was happening as she. She smiled for the first time in days and stepped out of the car and into his arms.

Dale cupped her face, his eyes nearly black with emotion.

"Okay, we'll see you inside," her mother called out, but Zoe couldn't look away, couldn't respond to anything else at this moment.

"I love you," he said.

"I know," she said. "I love you."

A beautiful smile lit up his face. "I know. We have to go in but let me…" he whispered and kissed her.

DALE TOOK HIS time and with his lips he tried to convey what he hadn't succeeded in telling her yesterday—how deeply he loved her, how desperately he wanted her, how serious he was about making her his.

Her eyes were bright, her smile brilliant when he lifted his head. For the first time, he noticed what she was wearing. He groaned out loud and grabbed her hand.

"You are looking so sexy. How the hell am I supposed to keep my hands to myself for a whole evening?" He growled and turned her around so he could look his fill.

SHE WAS WEARING a short, black lacy skirt with high-heeled boots that showed off her gorgeous legs. A soft pink top and a grey jacket rounded off the outfit. And from the look in his eyes, Dale clearly enjoyed the view.

"You can thank my mother." She giggled as he caught her in his arms.

"Hey," Don called from the door. "We want to start, come on!"

"On our way!" Dale said but didn't let her go.

"Dale, let's—"

"I want to show you why I haven't been sleeping lately," he smiled and pulled the pair of panties he'd taken from her bathroom halfway from his pocket.

"Dale!" She gasped and shoved it back. "Behave," she

scolded and kissed him.

"I don't want to," he said petulantly and didn't let go of her hand.

She stood on her toes. "Bend down, I want to tell you something."

Dale bent his head.

"I'm wearing a red pair. You can have them later," she whispered and his head jerked back.

He sucked in his breath and grabbed her elbow. "Let's get this over with," he whispered back. "I want to add that red one to my collection."

THE ONLY PEOPLE inside the restaurant were their families. Everyone except Hannah was there. A small sigh of regret escaped Zoe. It was obvious her mother and Dale's mother had plotted the evening, but what exactly was going on here she didn't know. She really wished Hannah was there, Zoe would've loved to share this magical night with her as well.

"What's going on here?" she asked Dale out of the corner of her mouth.

"You'll see." He smiled and ushered her forward.

The next moment she was swept up in Dale's mother's arms. "Zoe, I am so glad our Dale picked you." She sighed and cupped Zoe's face. "He's waited a long time for his soul mate," she whispered.

Zoe's eyes met Dale's over his mother's shoulder. Her

soul mate. Of course. That was the word.

"Zoe." Dale's dad smiled and kissed her forehead. "Welcome to the family."

"Well, come on, everybody. The smells from the kitchen are driving me crazy," Zoe's mother called out and took a chair.

Everyone else found a seat. Dale moved his close to Zoe's. She stole a glance at him. The glint in his eyes left her short of breath. He took her hand in his.

"We have bubbly—" Dale's dad began, but his wife interrupted him.

"That's only after—" She stopped speaking and looked at Dale.

"Am I on time?" Hannah called from behind her.

Zoe turned around. "Hannah?" she asked in amazement when her sister entered the restaurant, her suitcase trailing behind her.

"It helps if your brother-in-law has a plane." Hannah smiled.

Zoe jumped up and hugged her fiercely. "I so wished for you to be here and here you are. I'm so happy."

Dale bent forward and kissed Hannah. "I'm so glad you could come."

"There is no way I'd miss my sister's—"

"Hannah, come and sit, we haven't started yet," their mother interrupted Hannah and pointed to the chair next to Darryn.

Hannah hesitated for a second before she walked around the table. Zoe looked at Darryn. If he said anything nasty to her sister, she was going to kick him. But Darryn got up and bent over to kiss Hannah.

"Hi," he said and pulled out the chair for her. Hannah smiled at Zoe across the table and Zoe relaxed. She was thrilled that Hannah was here, but she knew how hard it was for her to be around Darryn. But it seemed as if she'd be okay.

Chapter Twenty-Two

P LEASED THAT EVERYONE who mattered in her life was gathered around her, Zoe leaned back in her chair. And saw that Dale was standing. Everyone else looked at her. Her breath caught in her throat. What in the world…

"If I can have everyone's attention…" Dale began and waited for everyone to stop talking.

He turned to look at Zoe. "It was right here in my mother's restaurant that I saw this woman for the first time," he said and laid his hand on Zoe's shoulder. "And although I didn't realize it at the time, I fell for her right there and then. It has taken me all these months to realize the reason why I can't sleep, can't focus on my work, forced her to do the interior decorating in our new hotel, jumped on a plane when I heard she was hurt, freaked out when I realized how much she's taken over my world, was because I love her."

While everyone laughed, Dale went down on one knee, and Zoe tried to gulp back the tears clogging up her throat.

"Zoe, I love you, and the part that I left out yesterday, the part that I thought was obvious but according to our mothers and Caitlin isn't, is that I want to spend the rest of my life with you. You've touched my soul, and I cannot imagine a day without you in it. Will you marry me?" With a grin, he flicked open the small box in his hand.

Zoe didn't look at the box, she stared into Dale's eyes. And it was there she saw what she'd been looking for so long—this guy was going to stay.

"Well, say something and put the poor sod out of his misery," Don hollered, and everyone laughed.

Zoe fell forward into Dale's arms and he lifted her up, laughing.

"Is that a yes?"

"Of course, it's yes, you idiot!" She laughed. "I was going to find you tomorrow to tell you that I only really registered what you said yesterday much later."

"You mean to tell me I could have had you without this circus?" Dale teased.

"Yes." She smiled. "But this is a wonderful bonus."

Dale bent down and kissed her.

"Your ring!" Dana cried out.

Dale lifted his head and laughed again. He took out the ring, for the first time looking a little bit uncertain. "If you don't like it, we can take it back."

The lump in her throat was the size of a golf ball and she couldn't talk. And those silly tears spilled over again. Dale took her hand and slid the ring over her finger. She sighed. He knew her so well. She wouldn't have chosen anything else. The ring was a beautiful vintage one in rose gold, covered in dozens of tiny diamonds.

He wiped her tears away with his thumbs. "If you don't like it—"

"I love it!" she exclaimed.

"But you're crying…"

"They do that when they're happy," Don said from across the table. "You still have a lot to learn. Can we now please open the bubbly?"

Corks popped, people laughed, glasses tinkled, but Zoe didn't really take any notice.

"Are you sure?" she asked.

Dale took both her hands in his. "I've never been as sure about anything before. But if you're still uncertain, I can promise you by the time the sun rises tomorrow there won't be a single doubt in your mind as to how I feel about you."

"I'M TAKING YOU to my house," Dale said when they finally drove away from his mother's restaurant.

Zoe nodded and put her hand on his leg. He brought her fingers to his lips.

"I'm very glad our mothers arranged tonight, glad everyone was there, glad you said yes, but now I'm especially glad I can have you all to myself," he said and put her hand back on his leg.

"So am I." Zoe moved her hand up and down his leg.

He stepped on the petrol and she giggled, moving her

hand higher and higher up his leg.

Turning onto the street where his house was situated, he grabbed her hand. They were only seconds away but even that felt too long.

"Damn it, woman," he growled and pressed the remote control that opened his garage. "You're going to pay for teasing me."

"Oh, yeah?" Zoe giggled and returned her hand to his leg.

Fortunately, they'd reached his house. He drove straight into the garage, jumped out, and went around to open the door for Zoe.

"I've never been here," Zoe said but didn't look around her. Her eyes were focused on his.

"I'm hoping you'll never leave again," he said and kissed her hard. "I can't wait another second for you, but not here…" He grabbed her hand and pulled her behind him until they were in the kitchen.

"Now." He growled and, pushing her up against the wall, slid his hands under her top so that he could finally touch her skin.

"Dale," she whispered and he kissed her. Her mouth was soft, moist and opened for him.

"I can't wait," he hissed and his hands slid up her thigh, lifting her skirt higher. His hand froze and he lifted his head.

"You're wearing a garter belt?" he whispered, and with a shy smile, she nodded. "Damn woman, you're killing me."

He groaned and pushed the skirt up over her hips. "The red panties." He breathed, his legs threatening to buckle under him.

Without taking his eyes from hers, he slipped a finger under the lace of the panties to find her wet for him. She gasped, her eyes dilating with desire.

With one tug, he ripped the panties away and his fingers found her core.

ZOE GRABBED HOLD of Dale's shoulders. "Dale." She breathed his name while his fingers brought her closer and closer to losing control. His lips closed over her breast of the soft material on her top and, whimpering his name, she was spun away.

When she opened her eyes, she was sagging against the wall, her skirt still bunched around her hips. Dale's eyes were on hers while he kicked his pants away.

"Bedroom?" she whispered.

"Later, I can't wait that long." Dale grunted and lifting her up again, he drove himself into her.

Gasping for breath, she folded her arms around him. That she could love with so much abandon, staggered her. Each beat of her heart sang his name. She wanted this man with every breath she took.

Time stood still, his hands moved over skin, and she spiralled away. She tried to concentrate, tried to make the moment last, but sensation after sensation bombarded her being until she was spun out of control and was transported to a place way beyond the stars.

Her legs refused to support her any longer and together they fell onto the soft carpet in front of the door, both breathing hard.

"I promise you, we'll get to the bed," he growled. "But let me kiss you again."

THEY DID EVENTUALLY make it to the bed. Sometime during the night, he turned to her.

"Do you need something?" he asked.

"Just you," she whispered and slid over him.

Dale pulled her up and hugged her tightly to him. She really didn't want anything else from him. She only wanted him.

Epilogue

FAIRY LIGHTS LINED the cement staircase that led all the way down to the tiny beach at the bottom. After days of late winter rain, it was a beautiful evening with clear skies and a calm sea.

Zoe smiled in spite of the tears threatening to spill over. She hugged her dad's arm as the music swelled and they began descending the stairs.

Her sisters and Dana took their places, and Dale moved forward while his brothers waited behind him. Everyone was barefoot.

She looked and found her mother who was openly crying, but appeared extremely happy. This was exactly the scene she'd described to Dale all those months ago.

Dale stared as Zoe came slowly down the stairs, smiling and talking to everyone on either side of the stairs. She looked beautiful in a satin gown with a lace-covered top. Her bouquet was made up of exquisite pink roses.

Finally, she looked down at him; he caught his breath and smiled. Her mother had been so right—he was falling in love with her all over again because, damn it, yes, all his smiles began with her.

The End

The Cavallo Brothers series

Book 1: *An Impossible Attraction*

Book 2: *An Irresistible Temptation*

Book 3: Coming soon

About the Author

I have been reading love stories for as long as I can remember and when I 'met' the classic authors like Jane Austen, Elizabeth Gaskell, Henry James The Brontë sisters, etc. during my Honours studies, I was hooked for life.

I married my college boyfriend and soul mate and after 43 years, 3 interesting and wonderful children and 3 beautiful grandchildren, he still makes me weak in the knees. We are fortunate to live in the picturesque little seaside village of Betty's Bay, South Africa with the ocean a block away and a beautiful mountain right behind us. And although life so far has not always been an easy ride, it has always been an exiting and interesting one!

I like the heroines in my stories to be beautiful, feisty, independent and headstrong. And the heroes must be strong but possess a generous amount of sensitivity. They are of course, also gorgeous! My stories typically incorporate the family background of the characters to better understand where they come from and who they are when we meet them in the story.

Thank you for reading

An Impossible Attraction

If you enjoyed this book, you can find more from all our great authors at TulePublishing.com, or from your favorite online retailer.

TULE
PUBLISHING